Walkaway

Walkaway

Alden R. Carter

Holiday House / *New York*

Library of Congress Cataloging-in-Publication Data

Carter, Alden R.
Walkaway / by Alden R. Carter.—1st ed.
p. cm.
Summary: Fifteen-year-old Andy, fed up with his alcoholic father and annoying older
brother, leaves their northern Wisconsin cabin on his version of a walkabout, leaving his
medications to combat depression, anxiety, and delusions behind.
ISBN 978-0-8234-2106-0 (hardcover)
[1. Mental illness—Fiction.   2. Forests and forestry—Fiction.   3. Alcoholism—Fiction.
4. Runaways—Fiction.   5. Survival—Fiction.   6. Fathers and sons—Fiction.
7. Family problems—Fiction.   8. Wisconsin—Fiction.]   I. Title.
PZ7.C2426Wal 2008
[Fic]—dc22
2008011433

For my friends
Leigh and Linda Aschbrenner

Acknowledgments

Many thanks to all who helped with *Walkaway,* particularly my editors Regina Griffin and Julie Amper; my wife, Carol; and my children, Brian and Siri. Although my family also fought the problem of the alcoholism of a parent, this novel is not autobiographical, and no character or event should be considered other than fictional.

Chapter 1

I'm between the car and the garage door. Dad's yelling at me to get the "damned door up," but it's ten times heavier than it ever was before. Mom's not paying attention because Sylvia's whining that she wants to go back to the movie. Dad's getting so mad that he gives me a nudge with the bumper. But I still can't budge the door, and he starts revving the Ford's engine.

The scene flashes and I'm outside my body, watching from inside the garage, as the car crashes through the door. For a second the picture freezes, and I can see everybody: Dad hunched over the wheel, Mom half turned to yell at Sylvia in the backseat, and that other me, spread-eagled against the hood.

The back of Mom's van blocks my view when the Ford slams against the back wall of the garage, the rear wheels lifting off the ground like Dad's driving a car out of a Roadrunner cartoon. And I know there's a tremendous crash, but for some reason I don't hear it.

You know those seconds between a lightning flash and the thunder? The lightning's already hit—maybe it's killed some poor guy on a golf course or blown a hole in a barn roof or exploded a tall pine deep in the forest—but it hasn't hit you. Still you tense, because you know the sound wave is coming straight at you at seven hundred and seventy miles an hour. You can crawl under the bed or hide under the basement steps, but it's going to find you. That's the feeling I have when I wake from the nightmare and lie sweating in the dark.

Sometimes I think I've been waiting for that crash my whole life. I haven't, of course, since it's not quite four years since the night Dad almost killed me. He'd come home from work already half in the bag. Mom gave him a dirty look. He waved it off. "Just relax, honey. Ned and I had a couple with a client at the end of a long week. No big deal. I'm fine."

Dinner seemed to sober him up, and he was cheerful until Mom announced that we were all going to the movies. (Not Rodge, of course, since he had his first girl-friend and was spending as little time with us as possible.) Dad sighed. "Laura, honey, I'm dog tired. I just want to sit, read the paper, and maybe have a fire in the fireplace. You go ahead and have a good time."

"Once a week I'd think you could spend a little time with your children."

"But I'm at home almost every night."

"School nights are different. Now, come on, or they'll be disappointed."

It didn't help that we went to the latest animated Disney movie. Dad kept shifting in his seat. Finally, he leaned over and whispered to me: "This movie is just for kids. I'll be next door."

We stayed for another half hour. Then Mom was up. "Let's go," she hissed. Sylvia whined, but Mom jerked her out of her seat by the arm.

Outside the Cock's Crow, Mom said, "Go in and get your father, Andrew."

"But, Mom—" She glared at me, and I pushed through the door into the long, smoky room. Dad was down at the end of the bar, a beer in his hand, laughing with a couple of guys. Another empty beer bottle and two empty shot glasses stood at his elbow.

I made my way through the drinkers and pulled at his coat sleeve. He looked down at me in irritation. "What? Is the movie out already?"

"Sylvia didn't like it. We left early."

"Well, there's a waste of good money! If you kids weren't going to like it, we could have rented a DVD and saved me a few bucks."

"I liked it fine," I said.

He ignored that and signaled the bartender. "Bill, give us another round down here."

The bartender served the three of them another round and took a couple of bills from the cash in front of Dad. The two guys lifted their beers to Dad. He waved off the thanks. "Drink hearty, boys." He tossed off the shot and drank half his beer in three swallows. "Well, boys, it looks like I've got to get the family home. I'll see you later."

He stumbled slightly getting off the barstool, muttered something about a slippery floor, and headed for the door.

Dad's got to be just about passed out before he'll let anybody else drive. That night he seemed okay, steady and deliberate. Mom didn't say a word all the way home. None of us did.

When we pulled into the driveway, Dad said, "Get the door, Andy."

I hopped out and set myself to give the mighty heave it takes to get the garage door up. That was when the Ford lurched forward, pinning me against the door, and Mom started screaming.

I guess Dad must have nodded off or simply forgotten what his right foot was doing. Either way, it was just a split second before he got his foot down on the brake again. Good thing, because another inch or two and the bumper would have splattered my knees against the door and left me waving my remaining limbs like the cockroach my buddy Dick thumbtacked to the bulletin board in the school cafeteria.

As it was, I was more squeezed than pinned. I managed to boost myself up onto the hood. My shoes wouldn't fit through the gap, so I pried them off against the bumper and swung my legs over the fender to drop to the cold pavement. Nothing to it.

Inside the car, Mom stopped trying to wrestle control of the wheel from Dad. "For God's sake, just shut off the car, Oscar!" she yelled.

Dad mumbled something.

"No, you are not putting this car in the garage! I'll do it later. Now get in the house before the neighbors see you making a fool of yourself again." She clambered out, dragging Sylvia behind her. "Are you all right, Andrew?" Her tone made it sound like I was more than a little to blame for the whole commotion. I nodded, afraid that I might sob like a little kid if I opened my mouth. I was suddenly aware of how cold my feet were. I squatted and reached under the car to retrieve my sneakers.

Mom was still ripping on Dad when we got in the house: "You almost killed your son!" she yelled.

Dad had his head down. "I'm sorry," he said. "My foot slipped. It was an accident."

"You are drunk, Oscar! Drunk and pathetic!"

I tried to say something: that it was no big deal or that it really hadn't been that close or that it didn't matter. But they weren't listening.

Sylvia had retreated to her room. She's smart that way: Don't say anything, don't make any noise, just get the hell out of the way as fast as possible. Passing her closed door, I heard her talking to her stuffed animals, telling them that everything was okay and not to pay any attention to the yelling downstairs.

I pulled my clothes off and huddled under the covers. When the yelling finally stopped and Mom and Dad came upstairs, I figured they'd come in to say something to me. But they didn't, and somehow that made the whole evening seem all the more my fault.

Chapter 2

The slam of the screen door wasn't car-crash or thunder-clap loud, but it was plenty loud enough to jerk me from sleep. "Roll out, boys! Daylight in the swamp!" Bern yelled, mimicking the wake-up call that once rang through Wisconsin logging camps. He started clattering around the kitchen. Dusty, supposedly my dog although he sleeps under Bern's bed in the guest cabin, came out onto the front porch, glanced with disinterest at me, and trotted back to the kitchen to see what he could cadge from Bern. I rolled out of bed and started pulling on my clothes.

I'd slept on the front porch in one of the swinging beds that hang on chains from the ceiling. Nice place to greet the morning, especially if you've got leisure enough to take it slow. But Bern believes in hitting the floor while the mist is still on the river and the dew on the trees. He grinned at me when I passed through the kitchen on my way to the bathroom. "Coffee will be ready in a minute. Kick your lazy-assed brother out of bed."

"That's your job," I said. "He ignores me."

By the time I got out of the bathroom, Bern was on the garage roof, his hammer making a quick *tap bang* as he set and drove nails into shingles. Rodge grumped his way into the kitchen, poured himself a cup of coffee, and glared with distaste at the toast and open jar of peanut butter on the table. He sighed, took a piece of toast, and said, "Well, come on, stupid. We've got work to do."

"My name's Andy," I said.

He grunted and headed for the roof. I diluted a cup of coffee with an equal amount of milk, added four spoonfuls of sugar, took my own piece of toast, and went to join the party.

They shingled all morning while I ran gofer. Every now and then, I'd climb to the roof to see if I could do something more exciting, like pound a nail or two, but Rodge soon had me running for something else they needed. Every now and then, Bern would throw a nail at Rodge. "Friday, big guy. Party tonight! Beer and fillies."

We paused for lunch and were well into the afternoon when I heard Dad's car bumping down the long drive through the woods and then the loud *thump* when he hit a chuckhole.

"Dumb bastard," Rodge muttered. "Why doesn't he slow down?" He drove a nail down hard and slid the next shingle into place.

The dark blue of the Ford appeared against a clump of balsams by the storage shed then disappeared again. "He'll be here in a minute," I called to Rodge. "You coming down?"

"I'm busy. You handle it this time."

The Ford reappeared, lurching to a stop at the far side of the yard. Dad sat, head bowed over the wheel for a long moment before putting the transmission into park. I let out a breath. At least he wasn't going to use a tree to stop the car this time. On the roof, Rodge and Bern kept hammering.

By the time I'd crossed the yard, Dad had labored out of the front seat and stood leaning against the car, getting a Camel lit. "Hey, Dad," I said.

"I thought I tol' you to fill that damned chuckhole."

He hadn't. "I'll get it this afternoon. How was the trip?"

"Andy, when I tell you to do something, you do it. I never have to tell your brother twice."

"Sorry, Dad."

He took a long drag, pushed off, and swayed toward the foot of the ladder. "Hey, boys. How's it goin'?"

Bern glanced at Rodge, but Rodge just muttered something I couldn't hear and slapped another shingle into place. Please, I thought, don't piss him off now.

"It's going good, Mr. C. Real good," Bern said.

Dad stood swaying at the foot of the ladder, waiting for more—a smile, a joke, some acknowledgment. Rodge kept his back to him.

Dusty chose that moment to come bounding out of the brush. With a joyous yelp, he leaped on Dad, his front paws landing squarely on Dad's stomach. Dad stumbled back, caught his balance, and aimed a kick at him. He missed. Dusty commenced jumping around him, barking. "Andy! Get this damned dog off me!"

"Dusty, come here!" I yelled. "Come on, boy!" As usual, he ignored me. Dad snatched a chunk of two-by-four from the picnic table and pitched it at him, losing his balance in the process and stumbling against a sawhorse. It tottered and, for a second, I thought they were both going over on top of Dusty. Dusty retrieved the chunk of two-by-four and galloped off to flop under a tree, where he got the wood between his front paws and started chewing.

"Why don't you train that beast, Andy?" Dad snapped.

I knew he was just covering his embarrassment.

Still the question stung because he knew how hard I'd worked with Dusty, including two obedience courses at the vocational school.

"I'm trying, Dad, but he's not very cooperative."

"Well, try harder!"

On the roof, Rodge said something to Bern, and Bern laughed. They kept working, but I could see them hiding grins. So could Dad, and that's what did it. He spun and headed for the car, face twisted with anger, hurt, and humiliation.

I caught up to him. "Where are you going, Dad?"

"Goin' back to Brunswick, where I've got friends. Haven't got any here."

"Dad, they were laughing at me, not you. Come into the lodge. I'll make you coffee and something to eat."

"I don't want any damned coffee."

"But, Dad, I want to show you the ferns I mounted. I think I've found nearly every kind around here."

"You still messing with those stupid plants? You're suppos' to be helping your brother."

"Dad, come into the house. I'll see if there's some ice cream."

"Ice cream," he snorted, though he loves the stuff.

He jerked open the car door. I thought desperately. "Dad, Brunswick's a hundred miles, and you must be tired after working all week."

"I know how far it is! And I am tired. Damned tired. But I'm not going to stick around here with a bunch of . . ." Words failed him.

"Dad, let's go down to Cattail's," I begged. "I haven't been out of here in a couple of days."

That was the ticket. Cattail's meant a drink, and he wanted one. "All right. All right. Get in."

Dusty saw the possibility of a car ride and pushed past me to jump onto the front seat beside Dad. "We're not taking that dog!"

I grabbed Dusty's collar and dragged him out and across the yard to his chain. Rodge and Bern had come down from the roof to get shingles. "Damn it, guys," I hissed. "He said he's driving home. But I've got him talked into going to Cattail's. When we get back, don't treat him like crap, huh?"

"Down to Cattail's to get him more drunk," Rodge said. "Real good, stupid. Just brilliant."

Dad honked the horn, and Bern stepped forward to take Dusty's collar. "I've got him, Andy. See if your dad will let you drive."

But by then Dad needed a drink too much to give me a driving lesson.

Dad and Cattail shook hands across the bar when we sat down. "Hey, Cattail," Dad said. "How's business?"

"Good. Could always be better, but it's been a good summer. A beer and a shot for you and a Coke for the boy?"

"Set 'em up," Dad said. "Alvin Anderssen and the crew around?"

"No, they've been cutting off a forty near Bayfield. Beer money for the winter. Clyde's been over at the homeplace by himself."

"Is he okay?"

"Oh, yeah. Was in yesterday. The horse trailer broke an axle, and Alvin hired a kid with a tractor to do the skidding."

"That's good. Clyde's getting old for that work anyway."

"So are the horses."

Dad laughed. "Remember the time Clyde got lost bringing them back overland from Lake Letourneau?"

"Do I ever. Only time I ever kept the place open all night. Even the sheriff was in here knocking back a couple by three in the morning."

Dad shoved the shot glass across the bar for a refill. "Yeah, that was a night. And all the while Clyde's curled up under a tree, fast asleep, just waiting for morning."

It was a famous story in local lore: everybody down at Cattail's getting hammered and periodically going out to drive a few back roads looking for Clyde. No one had been all that worried; it'd just been an excuse for a hell of a party.

We stayed at Cattail's for two hours. A few people came in, had a beer or bought a six-pack, but most of the time it was just Cattail, me, and Dad. Once or twice Cattail winked at me, just to let me know that he knew I was still there.

In the past year, I'd come to like Cattail again. I'd liked him when I was a real little kid. But then for years I'd thought he had it in for Dad. I didn't know exactly why, but it was something serious. Dad might laugh and talk with Cattail, but that was just show. Cattail was an enemy.

When I was eight, Rodge went off to summer camp for the first time, and Dad had more time for me than he usually did. We were up at the lodge one July afternoon with Mom and Sylvia when a canoe race came down the river. That was a first on our part of the river as far as anyone could remember. Canoe races are usually held on flat stretches of water, but there are three or four pretty good rapids between Cattail's and White Buck tavern, a dozen miles downstream. After the last few canoes disappeared around the bend where the old logging railroad used to cross, Dad got the idea that we should all drive down to the White Buck to see the end of the race. Mom wasn't enthusiastic. Sylvia needed her nap, and

Mom didn't want me "hanging around a barroom all afternoon."

Dad laughed. "The White Buck's got a game room. He'll have the time of his life. You can stay here, and we'll be back for supper."

I was hopping with excitement. "Come on, Mom. It's a guy thing." The "guy thing" was a phrase I'd heard Dad and Rodge use when they wanted to get away from the rest of us. Maybe now I was old enough to be one of the guys.

Grudgingly, she let us go. I rode beside Dad, talking a mile a minute about how I bet a lot of the canoes had turned over in the rapids and how maybe we'd have to go on a search for missing racers. Dad went along with the fantasy. We were having a good time.

At the White Buck, some other kids and I played video games and then went outside to play tag and hide-and-seek. The bar emptied when the racers came into sight upriver. The finish was pretty exciting, everybody on the shore shouting for their favorites. Then all the adults trooped back into the tavern to buy the racers drinks. Every once in a while, I'd go see what Dad was doing. He'd won one of the betting pools and was buying drinks and talking about the old days on the river. But that was okay; I was having fun, too.

We didn't leave until nearly suppertime. "Ride in

the back, Andy," Dad said. "Watch and see if anyone's chasing us."

"Who'd chase us, Dad?"

"Cattail. He's got it in for me."

That seemed odd to me, because I'd always thought Cattail and Dad were friends. But I was only eight, and I figured they'd had a fight.

I rode kneeling on the backseat, doing my best to see out the dusty rear window. I couldn't wear a seatbelt and do my job, so I left it off. Dad either didn't notice or didn't mind. He drove hunched over the wheel, going very fast up the gravel road to Lorraine. It was dry that summer, and cars threw up plumes of dust on the hilly road. A mile or so behind us, there was another car, and I gave Dad reports on whether it was gaining or falling back. Dad kept the hammer down, rocketing us north, the car occasionally fishtailing when we hit a soft spot in the road. I assumed, of course, that the car chasing us must be Cattail's. I wasn't worried about our speed or the swerves or the abrupt rise and fall of our car as we topped one of the hills. We were in a race, and we had to stay ahead because Cattail had it in for us.

I knew Dad had enemies—that we had enemies. Some nights when I crept into his bed, he'd talk in his sleep. Most of the time I couldn't understand much, but he'd seem real mad, muttering: "You bastard! I'm going to get you, you bastard!" Other times he'd call someone in his dream a "son of a bitch," but mostly it was: "You bastard! I'm going to get you, you bastard!" I'd lie awake, wondering who was after Dad. Now I knew that Cattail was one of them.

For years after that, I shied away from Cattail, even when he and Dad were talking like old friends. It wasn't until last summer, when I was in the hospital, that I finally figured out why Dad had wanted me in the backseat. It wasn't that complicated, really. He was drunk as a skunk and having enough trouble keeping the car on the road without a talkative eight-year-old beside him. So get in the backseat, Andy, and never mind about the seatbelt.

"Have you got that driver's license yet?" Cattail asked me.

"No, just my permit. I won't be sixteen until the fall."

"He getting the hang of it, Oz?"

Dad grinned. "Yeah, he's a good boy."

Behind us, the door opened, letting in a lean old man, his clothes patched and his cheeks stubbly with white. "Hey, Clyde," Cattail called.

Clyde smiled shyly. "H'lo, Cattail. Oz. Andy." He shook our hands and took his usual place at the end of the bar.

Alvin Anderssen and the rest of his crew scared me, but I liked Clyde. He might not shave every day and his clothes might be patched, but he never smelled bad and his boots were always oiled. (Dad said you could tell a good woodsman by his boots.) I'd seen Clyde at Cattail's a lot of nights. If there were kids in the bar with their parents or young women with their boyfriends, Clyde would give them money for the jukebox. Then, when he'd had enough to drink, he'd get up, do a little jig in his heavy boots, and go out to sleep in the truck until Alvin and the rest of the crew staggered out at the end of the evening.

Cattail joined Clyde, and they talked quietly for a moment. I overheard Cattail say, "Yep. The check came in the mail this morning. Barbara took it to the bank when she went into town. So you're fixed for another month."

Clyde smiled, ordered a beer, and gestured to the two of us. His Social Security check was safely in the bank and out of reach of Alvin and the crew. Cattail would keep the money on account, selling Clyde groceries, grain for the horses, and seed for his bird and squirrel feeders.

Cattail opened a bottle of beer for Clyde and brought another beer and another Coke down to us. Usually Dad buys the drinks for everyone, but it's a matter of pride for Clyde to buy him one now and then. Dad lifted his beer in thanks, and I imitated him with my Coke. Clyde lifted a hand in acknowledgment.

When the beers were gone, Dad had to buy back, of course, adding a shot for each of them, and it was another half hour before we finally left. By then Dad was almost too drunk to walk, and he let me drive back to the lodge. I was still pretty shaky behind the wheel and wondered what I'd say if a cop pulled us over. Would they take away my learner's permit for transporting a drunk? Maybe they'd fine Dad, even pull his driver's license.

Dad was nodding off by the time I got the Ford parked in the backyard. I helped him out and into the lodge, where I got him on one of the swinging beds on the front porch. He protested a bit, saying again that he was going to drive back to Brunswick: "Where I got real friends."

"Maybe you ought to have a nap first," I said. "You seem pretty tired."

"Don't need any damned nap," he said, but he didn't make a move to get up.

"Maybe you could just rest for a few minutes. I'm reading a book about the voyageurs. I could read a couple of the interesting parts to you."

"I guess that'd be okay."

I thought he was about ready to fall asleep, but by the time I got back with the book, he'd fired up a Camel and lay staring at the ceiling, knocking the ashes into an ashtray balanced on his stomach. When he lit another Camel off the butt of the first—an "uncouth habit" according to him—I knew he was building up to blow.

Bern saved me, coming onto the porch with Rodge slouching behind. Bern dropped into a chair, wiped his face with a bandanna, and grinned his billion-watt grin. "So, Mr. C., how are things in Brunswick?"

I've never seen anyone resist Bern's grin. Dad was no exception. His mood swung instantly and he smiled. "Pretty good, Bern. A couple of people asked about you."

"Oh, yeah? Who?"

They talked. Rodge and I listened. Dad couldn't get his sentences together very well, but Bern just kept smiling and asking questions. Finally, Dad started nodding off.

"Well, I guess the boss is about to chase me back up on that hot roof," Bern said. "We'll talk to you later Mr. C."

"Don' let him give ya a lot of shit. Or we'll take him to court." Dad laughed at his joke.

"Well, I'd have a heck of a lawyer, Mr. C."

Dad chuckled, pleased as anything.

When they'd left, he tried to get another cigarette going but gave it up. "Now there's a gen'lman. A gen'lman an' a scholar." He fell asleep.

A gentleman and a scholar. That is *the* compliment at Yale. Or so I've heard all my life from Dad and Mom. (Mom's a Wellesley grad, which is just about like going to Yale, I guess.) In a backwater like Brunswick, Wisconsin, we are different: representatives of a more cultured and refined way of life. In other words, incurable snobs. Mom and Dad laugh at anybody who doesn't have their education and put down other people's achievements. Rodge is afraid of the water and can barely swim, which means he never made Eagle Scout. So every kid in the troop who was pushing to make Eagle immediately got labeled a "merit-badge hound" by Mom and Dad.

Mom's actually worse than Dad when it comes to being a snob. Dad can unbend when he's up north. Mom can't. For her, it's always us and the peasantry. Frankly, I don't know where they get all the we're-better-than-them stuff. Dad's dad ran a hardware store and Mom's owned a shoe store. It's not like we're descendants of intellectual nobility or anything; they were just two bright kids who got into good schools. But don't tell them that.

Until last summer, when I had to go through a lot of individual and group therapy in the hospital, I pretty much bought into the idea that we were different. Now I think it's a load of crap. A boozer is a boozer, a screwed-up family is a screwed-up family, and a messed-up kid is a messed-up kid. It's just a matter of degree and what you want to do about it. I'm working on that part.

When I climbed back on the roof, Rodge and Bern had stapled a sheet of plastic over the unfinished part and were sitting in the shade with beers and cigarettes. Rodge already had a book open and was deep into it. He's always trying to get Bern interested in intellectual stuff, but Bern doesn't give a hoot. He's going to college next fall to be a forester. (I've got my doubts if he'll get through—too many girls and parties.) Meanwhile, Rodge will be making Mom and Dad proud as a first-year architecture student at Yale.

Me? My grades don't quite suck, but they're nothing to brag about, so I guess Yale's out. I could have been an Eagle Scout—I love the water—but I haven't been to a meeting in months. I tell myself every once in a while that I'll get working on it come fall, but I tell myself that about the grades, too. I don't care that much about anything, really. I read books, walk in the woods, and go fishing now and then. Otherwise I pretty much drift. And run gofer, of course.

Bern was gazing dreamily at the river. When I sat down next to him, he slapped my knee. "You done good, Andy."

"So did you. Thanks."

"No problem."

Rodge turned a page, ignoring us. I watched the river for a couple of minutes. "Rodge, what are we going to tell Mom if she calls tonight?"

"Nothing." He turned a page.

"But he's really bad this time."

"He's been bad ever since she left."

"But if he keeps driving drunk—"

Rodge snapped the book shut. "Look, stupid, just what do you expect me to tell her? That Dad's getting shit-faced while she's off helping her parents? Do you really think she needs to hear that a week after Gramps had heart surgery?"

"I just thought—"

"You just thought maybe she'd like to drop every-thing so she can rush home and take care of you."

"No."

He snorted. "The hell you didn't. Well, grow up. She knows what's going on. He fell off the wagon the day she left, and he'll drink hard until she gets back. Then they'll fight. If he's real bad, she'll stick him in rehab for a week or two. Then everyone can go back to walking on eggs until it starts all over again."

"I know."

"Well, that's good, because I was beginning to think that I was the only one paying attention."

Bern nudged me. "Drop it, Andy. He'll sleep for a while. Take a break." He looked over at Rodge. "Hey, *compadre,* you going to read that whole book or we gonna go?"

"Let me finish this chapter."

"Okay, but those babes ain't gonna wait forever."

"Where are you going?" I asked.

"Dance in town tonight," Bern said. "Gonna see if any of these north country fillies need a little loving." He winked at me.

"You can use the shower first," Rodge said. "I'll be down in a few minutes."

When Bern was gone, I asked, "But what about Dad?"

"What about him?"

"What do I tell him when he wakes up?"

"Tell him that we've gone to a dance. What's so tough about that?"

"I don't know. It's just that—"

"It's just that I'm the big brother, so I should stay home and take care of him."

"Kinda like that, I guess."

He closed the book, slowly this time, and gave me a long cool stare. "Just what the hell do you expect from me? Do you think babysitting him is all I've got to do in my life?"

"But I took care of him this afternoon."

"So now it's my turn?"

"Well, kind of, yeah."

"Do you think that makes us even? Do you want to compare numbers? Because it's not even close! I've been doing it a hell of a lot longer than you have. And I didn't take half of last summer off like you did. So get used to the load, stupid. Because I've got twenty-eight days left in this summer, and then I'm gone. I am outta here. And I mean permanently. I'll send birthday cards." He opened his book.

I had a lump in my throat, and it took me a minute to swallow it.

"Hey, Rodge," Bern yelled. "Shower's open. Get your ass down here."

Rodge marked his place and walked to the ladder.

"Rodge, is Mom coming back this time?"

"Beats me," he said. "I wouldn't. Don't forget your meds tonight. You going batshit is the last thing I need right now."

"I don't need it either."

"Yeah? Well, don't change your mind because next time I might just leave you under the house."

Chapter 3

After Rodge and Bern left, I fed Dusty, fried a couple of hot dogs for myself, and sat down to eat. For the first time all day, Dusty acted like I was alive, staring fixedly at me while I ate, a long string of saliva hanging from his chops. "You've already been fed." He wagged his tail and made the low growl he interprets as friendly. I threw him a piece of hot dog.

I had my guide to edible and medicinal plants open, but I couldn't get interested. Rodge was right: I had to toughen up. When Mom called, I'd have to cover for Dad. She couldn't do anything and didn't need the worry. Besides, I didn't want to get Dad mad at me by tattling like a little kid. Toughen up, Andy, I told myself, wishing I felt even a little tough.

I got my three bottles of pills from the medicine

cabinet, lined them up on the table, and sat staring at them for a while. I had a pill for depression, another for anxiety, and a third for delusions: more or less the blues, the jitters, and bullshitting yourself. I used to think that delusions were those scaly, crawly things that pop out of the unconsciousness of crazy people and go running around the floor and walls of padded cells. But according to the Net, those are hallucinations.

Delusions are ideas that people can't talk you out of, even when all the evidence is on their side. Say that you think you're a genius when your grades are all Fs, your IQ score is 50, and you can't tie your shoes. Still, you go on believing you're a genius even though you're fifteen and still in first grade. You are deluded, dude. You are no genius but one dumb flipper.

I'm not sold on the head meds, as the guys on the ward called them. Suppose you think an invisible man is putting invisible bugs in your padded cell. You can see him and the bugs because you have magic powers. Then you start taking the pill which makes you sane again. You realize there is no invisible man and that you have no magic powers. But then you see that the walls of your padded cell are still covered with bugs. They never were invisible; everybody could see them all the time. You were just the only one who gave a shit. Furthermore, there are a hell of a lot of 'em. And since you're terrified of bugs, you go crazy. Now did you come out ahead taking that pill?

That's why I don't like taking head meds. You never know exactly what's going to happen. I put the pills back in the medicine cabinet. Maybe later.

Mom called at seven-thirty. "How are things going, dear?" she asked.

"Okay. How's Gramps?"

"He's got a ways to go, but he's doing better every day."

"And Grams?"

"Oh, your sister keeps her busy. Sylvia's talking a mile a minute these days."

"That's different."

"Change of scene got her out of her shell, I guess. How's your father?"

"Okay. He's taking a nap right now."

That made her instantly suspicious. "Has he been drinking?"

"He said he was real tired after working all week."

"Don't cover up for him, Andy. Has he been drinking?"

"I guess he's had a couple."

"He never has just a couple. How bad is he?"

"Not too bad, I guess."

"Let me talk to Rodge."

"He's not here, Mom. He went with Bern to a dance in town."

"And left you alone with your drunken father." It was more a statement than a question.

"It's okay, Mom. Really, he's not too bad. I can handle it."

She sighed. "Well, you shouldn't have to."

I hadn't planned to say it, but it came out in a rush: "Rodge says he's not coming back after he goes to Yale."

There was a long pause before she said, "Well, maybe that'd be best. He's got a promising future ahead of him."

"I'd never do that, Mom. I'll always come home."

"I know you will, dear."

"I wish you were here," I said miserably, hating myself for not being stronger.

"I will be soon. You boys do the best you can. If your father gets too bad, call Ned. Maybe he can get him into rehab for a couple of weeks."

Call Ned? Dad's law partner was about the last person in the world I'd call.

She gave me the usual instructions about hiding Dad's car keys and matches.

"Sure, Mom."

I checked on Dad. He was lying on his back, breathing heavily through his mouth. I already had the car keys in my pocket, and the pack of matches on the bedside table was empty. I eased his glasses off and draped a blanket over him. Dusty flopped down under the bed, thumped his tail a couple of times, and closed his eyes. "C'mon, Dusty," I said. "Let's go for a walk." He opened an eye to consider me, and then closed it. I didn't push the idea. To heck with him.

Dad and Rodge can spend a weekend at the lodge and never get out of sight of the buildings. Me, I've got to move, and I know every deer path for a couple of miles around the lodge. Bern's like me that way, and he's taught me most of what I know about the woods. When he first pointed out some of the wild leeks that grow on the river's floodplain, I was fascinated. I got him to teach me all the other edible plants he knew and then started reading about foraging. It's not a hobby for everyone. There are some things out there that can make you very sick or very dead. (You're nuts if you pick wild mushrooms without a lot of training.) But if you like the challenge and like trying some tastes that you'll never find in the grocery store, it's great.

Bern and I still get out on a hike now and then, but mostly I go by myself. I don't mind being alone. In the woods, I'm safe. Some of the kids in Scouts asked me why I'm not afraid up here after dark. I'm just not. There's nothing to hurt you at night in the woods. There aren't any poisonous snakes around here. Unless you get between a mama black bear and her cubs or leave food lying around your camp, black bears could care less about giving you any crap. You'll hear coyotes yapping at night, but you'll almost never see one. The few wolves around are even shyer. Bern says he's seen a couple. I never have. So what's left? Just darkness, night sounds, and what your imagination can make of them.

I followed the ridge paralleling the river to where it dips to let Balsam Creek flow into the river from the west. It was getting on toward dusk, the shadows long and the thickets already dark. It's the best time to see animals, and I moved cautiously when I got close to the creek. Over the years a sandbar has formed downstream of the mouth, sweeping in an arc as the creek's sandy waters mix with the river's deep current. The bar rises above the surface and clumps of grass sprout after the spring flood. Deer come to drink there. Raccoons, muskrats, turtles, herons, and a dozen other animals and birds all use the bar. So if you don't come blundering through the woods, there's usually a pretty good chance of spotting something.

That evening a dozen crows were circling the bar, cawing, landing, and then taking off to circle again. One crow seemed to get maybe three feet off the ground before it was jerked back to earth. What the hey? I worked my way closer. A crow in a tree on the shore—

probably a lookout—spotted me and cawed a warning. The flock took off, flapping away this time, leaving the tethered bird to flop back into the grass. Crap. Some jerk had set a trap and the crow had a leg caught.

The world has a lot of crows, and I guess it wouldn't have been any ecological disaster if I'd left this one in the trap. Dad or Rodge, maybe even Bern, would have shrugged and called it bad luck for the crow. But I didn't like the thought of the crow waiting out there for an owl, raccoon, or fox to come along and end his misery. I followed the creek upstream to the ford. I rolled up my pants, shucked off my boots, stuffed my socks in the toes, and knotted the laces together so that I could hang them around my neck. I stepped into the stream, feeling for a hold with my toes, and edged carefully into the deeper water, the muddy bottom sucking at my feet.

The other crows hadn't come back by the time I made it to the bar. The trapped crow hopped disconsolately at the end of the chain anchoring the trap to a piece of driftwood. It's almost impossible to sneak up on a crow, and when I pushed through the alders and stepped onto the bar, he tried to take off. I squatted and waited for him to settle down. After a couple more tries, he gave up and fixed me with his dark, glittering eyes. "You stay calm for a minute, I'll get that trap off your foot."

He didn't reply and didn't cock his head like a dog.

His eyes stayed steady, unblinking, showing nothing. I edged forward a step and then another. That was too much for him, and he flapped into the air again with a harsh caw, tumbled, and fell. I could see now that it was a muskrat trap with a single spring, its jaws clamped high on his leg. When I set a foot on the anchor chain to hold the trap down, he started flopping desperately, and I was afraid he'd tear his foot off trying to get away. But then I got my right foot on the spring and pushed down so that the jaws fell open and he flew, the downdraft from his wings brushing my face.

I watched him wing downstream over the darkening river. He cawed a few times, and I suppose he could have been cawing a thanks, but I knew better. Animals aren't like that, and he was only calling for his friends, letting them know that he had risen, almost if not quite, from the dead.

I crossed again at the ford and followed the north side of the creek to our property line and into a red pine plantation planted by the Department of Natural Resources. The DNR hadn't thinned the plantation yet, and the going was harder there, the pines close together and grown well over my head so that I had to pick my way. But I'd done it a hundred times before, and I hit the town road just where I thought I would. I walked north until I reached our drive, following it down to the lodge as the stars started coming out.

Dad and Dusty hadn't changed position. In the bathroom, I checked myself over for ticks, found a couple, and flushed them down the toilet. I sat on the far end of the porch from Dad and read until my eyes started to droop. It was early yet, just past ten, but I got ready for bed anyway. I was only halfway through brushing my teeth when I heard a crash from the front porch.

When I got there, Dad had both hands on the table a few feet from his bed, an overturned chair lying beside it. "Where are my damned glasses?"

"On the table right in front of you, Dad."

"Jeez, I almost killed myself on that damned chair. Why don't you have the lights on?"

"You were sleeping, Dad. I didn't think you'd want the lights on."

He found his glasses and got a Camel going with a pack of matches from his pocket. "Is there anything to drink around here?"

"Coke, root beer, maybe a Sprite. I could make you some coffee."

"Don't be intentionally obtuse! You know what I mean."

I hesitated. "There's some beer."

"Bring me one. One for yourself if you want it."

I went. He'd managed to set the chair upright by the

time I got back. I opened the beer for him and sat drinking a Coke. He sucked down the Camel and drank the beer, his gaze fixed on the night beyond the screen. "Rodge and Bern went to a dance," I said.

"Where?"

"Chelles."

"Good for them. Young bucks should get out."

"Maybe I should have gone along."

He stubbed out the cigarette and went back to staring at the dark. "You can't always be tagging along, Andy. Your brother and Bern need some time to be eighteen."

"I'm no bother."

"Well, you would be if they found the right girls. You'll understand better when you start liking girls more."

"I like girls now."

"Not in the way I mean."

Oh, yeah? I thought. Bet I think about that *way* more than you do.

He tilted back the can to get the last few drops. "Let's go down to Cattail's. I need something stronger than beer."

"I was just about to go to bed, Dad. It's getting late."

He glanced at his watch. "Hell, it isn't ten-thirty yet. I'm going. You can come or stay."

"I'll come along," I said.

Dad's nap had put him in a better mood. He didn't say anything when we bumped through the chuckhole I still hadn't filled.

"Feels good to be up north," he said. "Damn, I get sick of town. What do you say we move up here? I'll hang out my shingle in Chelles, go in three or four times a week. You can go to the high school in Napier. Sylvia can go to the grade school. Your mom can get a job somewhere. Maybe do PR for the paper mill in Chelles. God knows they could use better press than they get."

It was an old fantasy. I'm not sure if he used it to get to sleep some nights, but I sure did. If we all lived together in the woods, maybe he wouldn't have to drink so much and Mom could stop being so tense and irritable. We could all get along, not having to worry about the neighbors. I prompted him. "How about when a blizzard comes along?"

"Well, we'll have to have plenty of wood. Should have at least six or seven cords cut and split before the snow flies. And I guess we'd better do some insulating. And we'll need to stockpile some food in case we get snowed in. You like keeping track of things. You can be in charge of the emergency larder. As long as we've got wood and food, we'll be snug enough."

"Suppose Sylvia and I can't get out to the highway to catch the school bus?" (This was my favorite part.)

36

"I guess you'll have to study at home. There isn't any shortage of books. You could probably get your diploma without ever going to school. Just take an exam."

"I'd like that."

"That's what you can do, then. At least that way there'll be somebody home to keep the fires going and water in the soup pot."

I could just imagine those long, cold days after Mom and Dad went to work and Sylvia caught the bus to school. (She loves school and wouldn't miss a day if you paid her.) I'd bring in wood, make myself some cocoa, and then curl up with a book before the stove. I'd read a couple of chapters of something I enjoyed, and then do something hard. I'd even get a math book, go back to the point where I stopped understanding, and work my way up to where I should be. I'd read the science textbook, too. Learn all those things Rodge and Dad talked about. I'd even study my French. (Boy, would I surprise the kids in Brunswick when I showed up speaking French like a native after almost flunking last year.) When I'd finished my school-work, I'd make myself some lunch and then strap on snowshoes and go for a walk on the frozen river. Then back to bring in a little more wood and get supper started. And when everyone came home, they'd be happy with the warmth, the smell of supper on the stove, and with me.

But the problem with fantasies is that they never

really hold together. Mom would never be happy living in the woods and working in a small town. Sylvia was already a crab a lot of the time, and without her friends and cable television she'd be horrible. And Dad wouldn't stay off the booze no matter where he was. But, for the moment, I wanted to keep the fantasy going. "Do you think Rodge will visit?" I asked.

"Aren't we including him this time?"

"I thought he'd want to be at Yale."

Dad nodded. "True. I hadn't considered that. Sure, he'll come home for vacations. Hell, you'll be so handy by the end of that first winter, you'll be bossing him around."

"That'd be a nice change."

"Don't let him get under your skin. I know he's bossy sometimes, but you'll get your turn someday."

Bossy sometimes? I'd take sometimes as an improvement. "Who exactly am I going to boss around?" I asked. "Sylvia? I'd like to see the day she does any work."

"She's still a little girl, Andy. She'll grow up. Here we are." He swung the Ford into an open parking space in Cattail's lot.

"Dad," I said, "could we really do it? Really move up here?"

He laughed. "Maybe someday." He swung the door open and headed for the tavern.

Chapter 4

Cattail's closed at one, and I drove us home. I hadn't driven much at night, so I took it easy. A mother skunk and three little ones hustled off the road and into the ditch, otherwise no wildlife. Rodge and Bern still weren't back, but Dad made no comment as he swayed off to the master bedroom. I washed up and then crawled into my bed on the front porch.

Rodge and Bern pulled in around two. They were in a good mood, maybe a little drunk, and laughing when the door of the guest cabin slammed behind them. I turned over and went back to sleep.

It was eight-thirty in the morning, the day already warm, before I opened my eyes. I smelled coffee and bacon. I grabbed my clothes and headed for the bathroom off the back porch. Dad was slicing potatoes into the big cast iron skillet he always uses to cook breakfast at the lodge. "Hey, Dad."

"Good morning. As soon as you've washed up and dressed, you can call the boys. Breakfast is just about ready."

I took a leak and then jumped in the shower. There's never a lot of hot water, so I made it quick. Besides, I was hungry. I dressed and trotted across to the guest cabin. Bern was up, but Rodge was still a lump under the covers in the bed against the far wall.

Bern had his Duluth pack open and was stuffing in spare clothes. "Hey, Bern," I said. "Are you off somewhere?"

"Yep. Met a couple of girls at the dance last night. They invited us up to their place near Storm Lake for a couple of days."

"Is Rodge going, too?"

"As of last night he was. I don't know about this morning."

"But how about the roof?"

"Oh, we're almost done. We can try to get the shingles on this morning or leave it until next week. It depends on your brother." He yelled: "That's if he ever gets his lazy ass out of bed!"

Rodge groaned and turned over. "Ten more minutes."

"Dad says to come right away if you want your breakfast hot."

Rodge groaned again but swung his feet over the side of the bed.

"How you doing, big guy?" Bern asked.

Rodge only grunted, levered himself up, grabbed his clothes, and headed for the shower.

"Ain't exactly a morning person, is he?" Bern grinned.

"Nope. Never has been."

We shared a laugh, which is one of the really good things about having Bern around: He laughs and makes other people laugh, even Mom. "So you'll be back Monday?" I asked.

"Monday late, maybe Tuesday. We'll see."

"But you are coming back."

He got the last flap on his knapsack secured. "Sure, I'll be back. I just don't want to name the day." He hesitated. "But, Andy, I've got to make some money for college. We're just about finished with the big stuff here. If there's a good job up there, I might just take it." He nudged me with an elbow. "Besides, Ol' Pete's been a little lonely and could use some action. And this girl's mighty fine and mighty willing."

"Is Rodge's, you know, willing?"

"His peter or his girl?"

"His girl."

Bern slipped into the drawl he likes to put on some-times. "Well, that you'll have to ask him, pardner. I wasn't paying too much attention."

On the back porch, Dad began ringing the big triangle that once called loggers to meals in a lumber camp.

Breakfast was nearly over when Rodge brought up their plans.

"Storm Lake, huh?" Dad said. "That's a nice area. Well, if you've got the garage buttoned up good, I don't see any problem."

Rodge glanced uncertainly at me. "I was thinking maybe you wouldn't want Andy here by himself."

"Oh, I'm going to stay for a few days. Ned's coming up tomorrow. We're going to work up a case and then go up to Longridge for the preliminary hearing on Wednesday."

I stared at him. We'd spent hours together yesterday, and he hadn't told me anything about him and Ned and a case in Longridge.

Dad and I got stuck with the dishes, of course, Dusty helping clean up the scraps. "Dad, do you suppose Dick could come up for a few days?"

"That wouldn't be a problem for me. I like Dick. How would he get here?"

"Well, I was thinking maybe his mom could give

him a ride as far as Kastrup, and we could pick him up there."

Dad grimaced. "That's fifty miles. I just got here yesterday. I don't want to waste half of today on the road."

Damn. "It was just an idea," I said.

He washed and I wiped for a couple of minutes. "Well, it's a pretty day," he said. "I guess I wouldn't mind a drive."

"Really?"

He smiled. "Go call him and see what you can arrange."

Everything went off without a hitch. Dick wanted to get out of town. His mother didn't mind the drive since she'd have a chance to see her sister in Thatcher on the way back. And Dad continued in his good mood.

We were a few miles on the road to Kastrup when Dad asked, "Are you still mad at Ned?"

"Uh, I didn't realize I was."

"Well, he wasn't very diplomatic when you two got in that argument about the Brewers."

"I still think I was right. We're not that far away from being a great team."

"Ned's seen a lot of baseball. And he played some in college. I think he might have had a point or two."

"Well, yeah. But he didn't have to tear down everything I said. I had a couple of points, too."

"I know. But he's a trial lawyer, and most of them are a little rough. Besides, he's got some problems at home."

This was new. "Oh, yeah? What are those?"

"His wife is an alcoholic. The maid they have is really there to keep her from drinking while Ned's at work. That's why he likes to cut loose a bit when he's up here." He reached over and slapped me on the leg. "Just the way I do."

The detector that occupies a cozy corner of my brain let out a squawk and began flashing red: *Alert! Alert! Incoming bullshit!*

"Uh, Dad, how exactly would you define alcoholic?"

He pursed his lips. "I guess I'd say it was somebody who couldn't get his work done because of drinking. But a real man—or a real woman, for that matter—can control it. I've had too much to drink more than a few times, but I've never missed a day of work because of it."

The shit detector blew a fuse in a puff of greenish smoke. Like hell! I thought. How about those times you were in detox or rehab? How about my birthday when you were too sick to get out of bed? Where do you think I've been all these years?

Dad went on like he hadn't just told one of the whoppers of the century. "And Ned may have a few drinks now and then, but he's always up and at it the next morning. Anyway, try to get along with him. He really is a good guy."

"Sure, Dad." Translation: I was going to stay as far away from Ned as I could. Not only is Ned Miller a jerk, he scares me. He's a big guy. His lips are thin and turn down at the corners like he's sucking on a lemon. He's got these suspicious little pig eyes like he knows you've done something wrong and he's damned well going to figure out what. He used to be district attorney, until he lost an election and went into practice with Dad. Some of his stories really creep me out. One time he got called to this house in the country where an old guy had blown his head off with a shotgun. Ned laughed telling us how a new sheriff's deputy puked when he saw the chickens pecking at the old guy's brains. I felt sorry for the deputy. I'm sure I would have puked if I'd seen that. My question was: Why hadn't Ned?

Beyond scaring me, I guess I dislike Ned because he screwed up the times Dad and I used to have alone at the lodge. Starting when I was around ten, Dad and I would go north on "bachelor weekends" four or five times during the winter. (Rodge was always too busy with friends and later girls.) We'd leave as soon as Dad got home from work on Friday, grabbing a burger on the way out of town, and getting up in "God's country" by eight or so. After the snow got deep, Dad would park on the town road, and we'd walk down the drive to the lodge. We'd get fires going and then go to the pump house for water. By the time we had enough water and wood in for the night, the kitchen would be warm enough for us to take off our coats and snowmobile suits. Dad would warm up a can of soup and make grilled cheese sandwiches and bacon or maybe pork chops and fried apples. And we'd talk.

Saturdays we'd eat a "lumberjack breakfast," do our chores, hike in the woods, and then hang around the kitchen because it was the warmest room in the lodge, reading our books or talking. With two or three hours of daylight left, I'd usually go out again on my own. By the time I was eleven I was pretty good on snowshoes, and there wasn't much of anywhere in a mile or two around the lodge that I didn't know by heart. The best part was the quiet. The breeze in the tops of the hemlocks, the plop of a lump of snow falling from a spruce bough, the chatter of a squirrel in a bare maple—somehow they were all only ripples in the silence of winter woods.

Dad would have a steak supper ready by the time I got back, and food never tastes so good as it does after you've been hiking in the cold. I'd tell Dad about my hike while we ate and maybe he'd tell a story about when he was a kid. After dinner, we'd read our books or Dad might read aloud. That was the best. Back then I didn't pay much attention to how much he drank. He never had more than a spike in his coffee in front of me. I suppose he did his serious drinking when I was off in the woods or after I'd gone to sleep. But what we did at the lodge was a "guy thing," and it never bothered me to lie when Mom quizzed me after we got home.

But then Ned started coming north with us and everything changed. Instead of cooking suppers at the lodge, we'd go to a restaurant in town, where they'd drink martinis while somebody else grilled our steaks. On the way back to the lodge, we'd hit the bars. I'd tag along, all the time missing the weekends it had been just Dad and me and walks out in the cold, silent woods.

Chapter 5

Dick was sitting at the counter in the Kastrup Café when we came in. He jumped up. "Hey, Mr. C." They shook hands. I waited my turn.

"Had your lunch, Dick?" Dad asked.

"No, I was waiting for you guys."

"Let's get a booth then." Dad led the way.

Dick slapped me on the shoulder. "How's it going, Andy?"

We ordered hamburgers, fries, Cokes for us, and a beer for Dad. We played the jukebox, and Dick flirted with a couple of high school girls who'd come in and taken a table near the door. I don't have the knack, so I studied the songs on the playlist until our hamburgers came and we headed back to the booth.

"Make any time?" Dad asked.

Dick grinned. "Oh, they were kind of tough, Mr. C. Said they were waiting for a couple of guys."

"Not you two, huh?"

"Not this time. Next time Andy can turn on the charm."

Dad laughed a little too hard at that. They talked while we ate. I didn't mind. Dick always has more to say than I do.

Dick's been my best friend just about forever. Our moms used to stroller us around the block together when we were babies, and I think he knows me better than anyone. When things started getting rough for me a couple of years ago, a lot of my friends sort of edged away, embarrassed or afraid they'd get infected or something, but Dick was always my friend. Last summer, when I was in the hospital, he wrote me every few days to update me on what was going on back in Brunswick. Of course, Dad's drinking is no secret to Dick. Not that I talk to him about it, since that would break Mom's code of silence about never, ever telling the neighbors (or anyone else) because "Your father's a professional person."

Dad likes Dick, calls him "the most mature" of my friends. Dick just eats that up because he's always been in a big hurry to grow up. They kept the conversation going all the way back to the lodge. Dad even went so far as to tell us a little about the case he and Ned were working on, although usually he's real tight-lipped about that sort of thing.

At the lodge, Dick and I got our fishing gear together. Dick invited Dad to go along, but he said he was going to putter around the place for a while. When we were getting some pop from the refrigerator, Dick said, "Do you suppose he'd mind if we took a couple of these beers?"

"I don't know. I guess you'd have to ask him."

And he did, coming back a couple of minutes later: "Allll right. He said no problem as long as we asked first." He put a couple of cans in the cooler.

"I don't really want one," I said.

"Suits me. I'll drink two."

In the boat, Dick primed the outboard, set the choke expertly, and got it going on the second pull. "I wish I could get it started that easy," I said.

"It's all in the wrist," he said. "Watch next time and be amazed."

We motored upstream under the highway bridge, past Cattail's, and then under the old one-lane bridge that had carried the highway years ago. About a mile above the old bridge, the river splits around a swampy island that's a few inches above water in normal water and all but disappears when the river runs high. "Which side shall we take?" Dick asked.

"Take the right channel. We'll go to the top of the island and then float down past the Old Maid's."

"Who's the Old Maid?"

"Oh, she's this weird old lady who's got a shack on the riverbank. Rumor is that she's a retired whore."

"Wait a second. Isn't an old maid a woman who's never had sex?"

"Never been married anyway. I don't know why they call her that. No one sees her much. There's this old guy who works with Alvin Anderssen named Clyde Penningford. He brings her groceries every couple of weeks, gets drunk with her, and stays the night."

"Penningford? That's quite a handle for an old lumberjack."

"Yeah. Dad jokes that Clyde's the black-sheep son of an English lord."

"Weirder things have happened, I guess. That the Old Maid's shack?"

"That's it."

"And she actually lives in that dump?"

"Yep. There she is now."

"Where?"

"Out behind in her garden."

The Old Maid must have heard our motor because she straightened then: a heavy old woman in suspenders, patched trousers, checked wool shirt, and a floppy felt hat. She glared at us.

"Eeeyuck," Dick said. "Imagine being trapped for a winter with her."

"No, thanks. I used to have nightmares about her when I was a kid." I lifted a hand and waved. She didn't wave back.

"I don't think she likes us on her river. Let's drift down the other side of the island."

When we'd turned the upstream end of the island, Dick shut off the motor, and I tied off the anchor so that it bounced along the bottom. We drifted with the current. Dick pulled out his cell phone and checked for messages.

"Forget it," I said. "Cell phones still don't work up here."

He cast his line and lit a cigarette. "Want one?"

"I'm trying to quit."

"Been ripping off a lot of your old man's Camels?"

"No," I said. "Those are way too strong."

"I wish my old man smoked menthols. I really like those."

"Yeah, they're okay," I said. (Actually, I thought they all tasted like crap, but I didn't want to sound like a wuss.)

"So, any girls around this summer?"

"I saw a couple in Cattail's the other day, but they were a little too old for us, I think."

"There ain't no such thing for me. At least if they're younger than twenty-five or so."

"Don't you wish," I said.

"Actually, I was dancing with this older girl the other night. She told me she was going to be eighteen in September."

"How old did you tell her you were?"

"I told her I was seventeen."

"She'll know you're a liar when we're sophomores in the fall."

"Nah. She's from Chippewa."

"Did you get a date?"

"I got her number. But I don't know. She wasn't really my type. I've been hanging around with Melody Jenkins. I wouldn't have come up here if she hadn't been going on vacation this week. The babe is definitely hot for me." A fish interrupted him. Or at least he thought it was a fish until his line refused to move. "Oh, hell," he said. "I'm snagged. Get the anchor up. I don't want to lose this lure."

He fed out line while I got the anchor up, fitted the oars in the locks, and rowed up the line until he was able to free his lure. "Got it. So where are Bern and Rodge?" he asked.

"Up in Storm Lake visiting a couple of girls."

"I guess I should have come up a day earlier. We

could have tagged along. Where there are two girls, there are bound to be more."

"Rodge would have ditched us the first chance he got and let us walk home."

"Nah. I get along fine with your brother."

"Good for you."

"Is he still giving you a rough time?"

"Same old, same old."

"Still the gofer, huh?"

"You got it."

"How's the Mountain Man?"

"Bern? He's great. Last week the two of us put together survival kits."

"What for?"

"For fun. Bern read this article in *Outdoor Life* and thought it'd be a cool thing to do."

"What do they look like?"

"Everything fits in a Sierra cup with a folding handle and a watertight lid. You can cook wild plants in it or boil water so you don't get giardia."

"What's giardia?"

"It's this parasite in the water. Bern calls it beaver fever because beaver crap spreads it. It gives you a major case of the runs."

"Delightful. Remind me never to go swimming again."

"Just don't swallow the water. Anyway, the cups

have these cases you can hang on your belt. In mine I've got a compass, matches, one of those keychain lights, bandages, antiseptic, bug dope, fish hooks, a couple of sinkers, a real small bobber, some line, a little container of salt—"

"Salt? What for?"

"Bern says you've got to have some salt in your diet to stay healthy. Besides, fish tastes better if you've got a little salt. I've already used it a couple of times."

"You got lost and had to fish for your supper?"

"Not exactly. Bern and I decided to try fishing Huck Finn-style. So we went down to Balsam Creek, cut a couple of branches, put on tackle from our kits, and actually caught a couple of fish. Bern said we ought to try them raw like sushi, but I talked him into starting a fire. We roasted them on our fishing poles."

"Whole?"

"That's another thing I talked him out of. We cleaned them using Bern's Leatherman."

"What's a Leatherman?"

"It's this really cool survival tool. It opens up into pliers and then there are a bunch of different blades that fold out of the handles. Kind of a super Boy Scout knife. I blew half my money on one the next day." I felt for the leather case on my belt, unsnapped it, and handed him the Leatherman. "Don't drop it in the river."

"Wouldn't think of it. Hey, this is cool." He started unfolding blades.

We'd floated under the old bridge and almost to the boat landing on the west bank above the highway bridge. "I guess you'd better start the motor," I said. "We don't want to hit one of the bridge pilings."

Dick snapped the blades of the Leatherman shut and handed it to me. There was a plop just off the stern and a widening circle of ripples. "What the heck?" Dick said.

"Probably a fish rising."

"Couldn't be. There's something floating. . . . Hey, watch out!"

We both ducked as half a dozen pinecones showered around the boat. "We're under attack, Captain!" I yelled as three girls in swimsuits charged onto the landing and let go another barrage of cones.

"Return fire!" Dick yelled.

We started grabbing cones from the bottom of the boat and firing them back. They mostly fell short since we were throwing from our seats while they could get their whole bodies into it. "We have to retreat," I shouted.

"We're the navy! We never retreat! Up anchor, get ready to land. We shall revenge this sneak attack." Dick let out a wolf howl, pulled the starter rope, and swung us around as I got the anchor aboard.

The girls were scrambling around for more ammunition. A blonde, taller and probably older than the other two, ordered them to hold their fire. "We're in for it now," I said.

"I get the blonde. You can have your choice of the other two. Duck!"

The girls charged again and started heaving pinecones as fast as they could. A cone bounced off my head, and I took a couple more hits to the body before the girls ran out of ammunition. They ran.

"Hey!" Dick yelled. "Don't run. You've got to answer for this."

The blonde looked over her shoulder, grinning. "You've got to catch us first!"

Dick cut the engine and pulled up the prop. By the time we'd drifted the last few feet to shore, they'd disappeared into the woods. We scrambled out. "Come on, guys," Dick shouted. "Let's have a truce."

We heard giggles and a little argument and then the three edged out of the bushes. "Really a truce?" the blonde called. "We don't want to get thrown in the river or anything."

Dick made the Boy Scout sign. "Scout's honor."

"How about your buddy?"

"Me too," I called. "You're safe."

They came down to us. Up close, the blonde and the pudgy brunette looked about our age. The skinny girl hanging back a little was definitely younger. Dick stuck out a hand to the blonde. "I'm Dick. This is Andy."

"I'm Crystal. This is Sonia and that's Izzy."

Dick got right to the point. "So, how old are you guys?"

"Sonia and I are sixteen," Crystal said. Izzy snorted. "Well, almost. We're fifteen. Izzy's fourteen."

"Almost?" Dick grinned.

Izzy was apparently the truthful type. "I'm thirteen," she said. "I won't be fourteen until November."

"How about you guys?" Crystal said.

"We're both sixteen," Dick said.

"He is," I said. "I'm one of the almosts."

I figured that should get a giggle or at least an acknowledgment of my honest and forthright character. No such luck. Dick had the charm turned up to full blast, leaving Crystal and Sonia pretty much mesmerized. Only Izzy seemed immune. I was tired of holding the boat, so I got the anchor out of the bow and wedged it behind a rock at the edge of the landing.

"You guys sisters?" Dick asked.

Sonia was determined to get into the conversation. "Cousins. Our three moms are sisters. Every year they have a women's retreat. This year they rented a cabin at Cattail's and dragged us along."

"Big bore, huh?" Dick asked.

Crystal and Sonia giggled. "It was until a few minutes ago," Crystal said. Izzy rolled her eyes and then ran fingers through her hair and started adjusting her ponytail. I noticed that she hadn't started shaving yet, or that she'd forgotten for a while. Sonia stepped over to her and whispered something. Izzy pulled down her arms, her cheeks turning red. I made like I hadn't noticed, but she must have caught me looking. She turned quickly and headed for the highway bridge.

"Where you going, Izzy?" Crystal called.

"Back to the cabin. I'll see you guys later."

"What happened?" Crystal asked.

Sonia pinkened a little herself. "Tell you later."

"Oh, I bet I know. She was showing her hairy pits, huh?"

Sonia made a face. "Yeah. We've got to talk to that girl again."

The subject of intimate grooming didn't seem to faze Crystal. She grinned at us. "Izzy hasn't gotten around to some big-girl stuff yet. She's still kind of a tomboy."

We talked for another half hour. Or the three of them did and I listened. Dick tried to talk them into a boat ride, but they said "The Moms" would get upset if they didn't ask permission first. "We gotta go," Crystal said. "Maybe we'll see you later."

"Come down to the picnic area across from Cattail's when it starts getting dark," Dick said. "We'll have a fire and push you on the swings."

We got the bow off the shore and headed for home. "Well, that puts a different spin on the ol' evening," Dick said.

"For you maybe. That Sonia girl didn't say a word to me."

"You've got to take the initiative, son. Ain't I taught you nothin'?"

"Not much. Besides, she probably weighs more than I do."

"So what? It's not like you're going to hang out with her forever."

Dad was on the front porch with a cigarette and a martini. "Catch supper for us?"

"It was frustrating, Mr. C.," Dick said. "We got half a dozen hooked good, but every darned one of them was too big to haul into the boat."

"Actually, he was more interested in hooking this blonde," I said.

"Oh, yeah? Where'd you meet her?"

Dick told the story of the pinecone attack.

Dad laughed. "So how'd you do, Andy?"

I shook my head. "Not so hot. Dick grabbed the blonde, leaving me to choose between the fat one and a thirteen-year-old."

Dad laughed again and went to put steaks on the grill out back. Dick and I set the table on the front porch. "You oughtn't to put yourself down like that," Dick said. "Sonia isn't that bad. You can hang around with her for an evening at least."

"What do I talk to her about? Weight Watchers?"

"Negative, negative, negative. She might turn out to be fun if you give her a chance."

"I gave her plenty of chances. She never even looked at me."

"That's because you never acted like you were interested."

Because I'm not, I could have said. But the truth was I would have been happy to talk to her or even Izzy. I just didn't know how.

Dad had another martini with his dinner and then went down to the river to cast for muskie before dark. We did the dishes. Dick was full of plans about how we could get somewhere with Crystal and Sonia. I mostly listened.

When Dad came up from the river, he asked us if we'd like to go to Cattail's or build a fire in the fireplace. "Cattail's," Dick answered before I could say anything.

Alvin Anderssen's battered three-quarter-ton pickup was parked near the door to Cattail's when we pulled in. "Looks like Alvin and the crew got back from Bayfield," Dad said.

Dad's step had a bounce when he went into the bar. Dick and I crossed the road and sat on the swings in the picnic area. "Who's Alvin?" Dick asked.

"Alvin Anderssen. Dad's known him and his brother for years. And Clyde, their hired hand. The one who takes groceries to the Old Maid. They cut pulp for a living. Alvin's wife, Nancy, works right along with them. Dad calls them the last of the hemlock savages."

"Meaning?"

"They only work when they have to. Otherwise, they drink beer, fish, and shoot deer. You should see the pile of beer cans outside their place. Every spring, Nancy takes about thirty bags of them to the recycling center. Dad says the cans are their bank account."

"No kids?"

"I don't think they ever had any."

"Hey, maybe if Sonia doesn't work out for you, you could see if that Nancy babe is interested in breaking in a young stud."

"You don't have the picture. She's probably fifty, washes her hair once a year, and changes her clothes maybe twice. Believe me, close to her you do not want to get. And, by the way, she's real friendly to everything in pants."

"Well, it was a thought."

"Not a good one. So, do you think Crystal and Sonia are going to come or not?"

"Give it a while. Let's start a fire."

We set about gathering sticks. The girls, all three of them plus one of The Moms, showed up half an hour later. I guess this mom had come along to make sure we weren't a couple of biker types or worse. She quizzed us in a nice sort of way for a few minutes and then got up to leave. "Don't stay out too late, girls. Are you coming, Izzy?"

Izzy was kneeling by the fire, absorbed in feeding in small twigs. She looked up. "Do I have to, Mom?"

Her mom hesitated. "Come talk to me." At the edge of the woods she delivered a few quick, emphatic sentences in a whisper. Izzy hung her head and nodded.

I kind of figured Sonia would drift my way once Dick and Crystal got talking. I'd even practiced some small talk for the occasion. I should have saved myself the trouble. Dick was pushing Crystal on a swing, and Sonia was waiting her turn. I left Izzy by the fire and wandered over. "Do you want me to push you?" I asked Sonia. "There's another swing."

"That seat's cracked. I'll wait my turn on this one."

"Oh, okay." I thought desperately. "Would you like

to roast some marshmallows? I was going across the street to buy some."

"Maybe later. I don't want to miss my turn on the swing."

I crossed the street to buy the marshmallows. Inside, Dad was sitting at the bar, buying drinks for Alvin and the crew. Nancy was next to him, swigging a beer. I'd seen the scene before: big-shot lawyer proving he's a man of the people by standing for all the booze. Classy, Dad.

Cattail sold me the marshmallows. "How are my great-nieces doing?"

"Your great-nieces? Sorry, I didn't know that part."

"They're good girls." He winked at me. "Treat 'em right. Just a sec, I'll get you some pop." He brought back a twelve-pack. "Tossed in a few of everything."

"Thanks, Cattail."

When I got back to the fire, Izzy was sharpening a marshmallow stick with a pocketknife. Four sharpened sticks already stood tilted against the log behind her. "Hey, good job," I said. "That'll save some time."

She closed the knife expertly and shoved it into a pocket of her jeans. "Thought I'd better make myself useful. Mom thinks I'm just in the way."

I glanced at the swing, where Dick was still pushing Crystal and Sonia was looking increasingly pissed off.

"Don't worry," Izzy said. "I'll know when to leave."

"Don't worry about it," I said. "I don't think Sonia likes me much."

"And I'm too young for you."

"I didn't say that."

"I didn't say you did. I am too young. You're going to be sixteen, I'm going to be fourteen. That's a lot."

"I guess," I said. "Can I use a stick?"

"If I can have a marshmallow."

"Oh, yeah. Sure."

The others joined us a few minutes later. Crystal and Sonia stayed on the other side of the fire with Dick, although as far as I could tell Dick wasn't giving Sonia any encouragement at all. After a couple of marshmallows, Crystal hopped up. "Come on, Dick. Let's go for a walk."

"But I want a push on the swing," Sonia bleated.

"Oh, we're done with that now. Come on, Dick."

And Sonia blew. She jumped up and yelled, "You always get what you want! I hate you!" She bolted for the path through the woods to their cabin.

Dick started to say something, but Crystal looped her arm through his. "Ignore her. She got her period today. Let's go."

Izzy and I were left sitting by the fire. "Wow!" I said.

"Forget it. They're always fighting."

"Over boys?"

"Over anything. This morning it was who has bigger boobs."

I laughed. "You say just about anything you want to, don't you?"

"Pretty much. It drives Mom crazy. I guess I'm going to have to work on being ladylike. But I figure, hey, I'm thirteen. I hardly have any boobs of my own—or at least nothing that a guy would notice—so who am I trying to impress? So I say what I want to."

"Don't change."

She glanced at me. "Why do you say that?"

"I hate being lied to. Around our house, everybody spends more time lying than telling the truth. For a while, it just about drove me nuts. Literally."

She peeled bark off her marshmallow stick. "So, you got trouble at home, huh?"

I shifted uncomfortably. "Something like that."

"So do we. That's the real reason we're up here. Mom and her sisters are having a big conference about whether she should divorce Dad."

"I'm sorry."

She shrugged. "Well, Dad hasn't been around much in the last few years. Mom's sisters are just helping her get courage up to file the papers. They're drinking wine and talking about what a big jerk Dad is and always was."

"So when are you going back home?"

"They're all leaving tomorrow. I'm staying up here for a couple of weeks while Mom gets things worked out in Milwaukee. I don't mind. Irma and Cattail are Mom's aunt and uncle. I can help Aunt Irma clean cabins."

We talked about the woods, school, music—all sorts of stuff. I tried not to be boring, but then got started talking about foraging. After a couple of minutes, I caught myself. "I guess you're not interested in any of this stuff, are you?"

She was watching me with her big blue eyes. "It's interesting to hear you talk about it. Most of the time you look real serious, like you're worried about something. But you kind of light up when you talk about being out in the woods. Are you also a hunter?"

I made a face. "No, I don't like killing things. Dad hunted when he was younger, and he tried to get Rodge and me interested but it didn't work out."

"Who's Rodge?"

"My older brother. He's up in Storm Lake with a friend for a few days."

"He doesn't like killing things either?"

I shrugged. "I don't think he gives a damn. He'll shoot a squirrel, a woodchuck, or a porcupine around the place, but he says that he lacks the patience to really hunt."

"And that was okay with your dad?"

"I guess so. But Dad got real mad at me for getting upset after I shot a chipmunk."

"Why'd you shoot a chipmunk?"

"To see if I could hit. And I guess to make Dad proud of me. But I felt really bad afterward. I mean that chipmunk wasn't doing any harm, and I didn't have any right to kill him. I haven't shot anything since. . . . I guess that makes me sound like a wuss."

"I don't think so. I think it's awful what we do to animals. I'd be a vegetarian if Mom would let me, but she says I have to get my growth first."

"Do you like being up north?"

"I love it. The air smells so good and it's so peaceful, so much better than stinky old Milwaukee with all the traffic and people shooting each other on Saturday nights. My mom's really paranoid about letting me go anywhere. I wish I lived up here."

"So do I."

"Why?"

"Same sort of reasons. I mean, Brunswick doesn't have the traffic, but we've got this paper mill and . . ." I paused. She was grinning at me. "Wait a second. What are you laughing about?"

"Oh, nothing."

"No, come on, tell me."

She shrugged. "Oh, it's just that you said you wanted me to live up here. Like, you know, you wanted me around."

I thought back quickly. "Oh, I get it. I meant—"

"I know what you meant. I'm just teasing."

"I thought you didn't go in for that kind of thing."

She made a face. "Oh, am I spoiling my tomboy image?"

I laughed. "No, I'm just teasing you back."

She took a last swallow from her can. "Well, I guess I'd better get back. . . . That's unless you'd like to walk up on the old bridge and look at the moon."

I guess I hesitated a second too long on that one, because she hopped up. "Well, thanks for the marshmallows."

"No, wait a second. We can walk up on the bridge."

"It's okay. I know I'm too young for you."

I caught her hand before she could turn away. "No, really. I'd like to go up there with you."

Both of us stared down at our hands, which had somehow gotten firmly locked together. She pursed her lips and then leaned back to pull me to my feet. "Well, let's go then."

We started for the bridge, still holding hands. "I was

just kind of wondering when my dad would come out of the bar," I said. "That's all."

"Will he be upset if you're not around?"

"Oh, not really, I guess. He'll just go back in for another drink."

After a minute she said, "I'm sorry I started to run away. I'm not really like Sonia. I don't get mad just for the heck of it. Or because some guy doesn't push me on a swing or something."

"I'm sorry she had a bad time tonight. But I'm not sorry I got a chance to talk to you."

She squeezed my hand. "Yeah, you're a good guy to talk to. I just wish I were a little older. I hate being thirteen and looking like I'm ten."

"I don't think you look that young."

We skirted the mound of gravel that keeps cars from crossing the bridge while leaving enough space for four-wheelers and snowmobiles. The skeleton of the bridge rose around us and our footsteps echoed on the old iron. "Watch your step," I said. "The pavement's pretty crappy."

"I like this old bridge. It's really different."

"Dad says it's an arched-truss bridge and that it's close to a hundred years old."

"Really? That's neat."

At the middle of the bridge, we leaned on the rail and watched the long trace of moonlight rippling on the river. She started to say something, hesitated, and tried again. "Can I ask you something?"

"Sure. I guess."

"If I were older, would you try to kiss me now?"

"Uh, yeah. I guess. I mean, I'd want to."

She didn't say anything for a moment. "So would you?"

"Pretend that you're older?"

"And kiss me. I mean, I won't attack you or anything. I just want to see what it's like. And I took a shower and shaved this afternoon, so it's okay, you know, to put your arms around me and stuff."

I hesitated. "I'm no expert at kissing, so don't expect too much."

"Okay." She got up on tiptoes, shut her eyes tight, and puckered her lips. She looked kind of funny. I was so nervous I almost laughed. I leaned forward and gave her a quick kiss. It was over in half a second. She dropped to the flats of her feet and frowned.

"I warned you not to expect too much."

"No, it was okay. I guess I didn't know quite what to expect. Crystal and Sonia are always talking about kissing, and I just wanted to see what the big deal was."

I hesitated. "I think maybe it helps if you don't screw your face up." I did my best to imitate her.

"I did that?"

"Uh-huh."

She laughed. "Oh, God, that's embarrassing. Did I really look that bad?"

"Not bad. Just kind of nervous."

She squared her shoulders and took a breath. "Okay, I'm ready. . . . That's if it's okay."

"It's okay." I leaned down and did a better job. Her lips tasted of marshmallows.

She leaned back and looked at me. "That was better. I think I kind of see what they're talking about now. Thanks."

"Sure. I mean, thank you."

"I really ought to get back. Mom's going to start worrying."

She took my hand again as we walked down the bridge. "What are you thinking?" I asked.

"Oh, I was just thinking that when I'm sixteen, you're going to be eighteen. I wonder if I'll still be too young for you then."

"You'll meet lots of guys you can kiss before then."

"I suppose, but I'll still remember tonight. Especially screwing my face up like that for my first big kiss. How embarrassing!"

"Why don't you remember the second one instead?"

"Okay."

At the driveway leading from the road to her cabin,

she let go my hand. "Thanks for pretending I was a little older."

"No problem."

She hopped up on her tiptoes and gave me a quick kiss on the cheek. "See you," she said, and ran up the drive toward the cabin.

Back at the picnic area, I added some sticks to our fire. I felt good and kind of grown up. I mean, Izzy really was too young for me. Even had a little-girl nickname still. Soon she'd make everybody call her Isabelle, or whatever Izzy stood for. But it'd been fun to feel older and like I really knew some stuff.

Dick and Crystal came back twenty minutes later. They both looked a little breathless. They spent a long minute saying good-bye before she hurried up the path. Dick sat down beside me, dug a can of pop out of the carton, and said, "Wow!"

"That good, huh?"

"Oh, yeah. Way better than good."

I'm sure that he would have told me the details, but Dad came out of the bar then. He lit a cigarette and looked around. "Over here, Dad," I called.

He sauntered over. "Whew! Nancy was getting a little too friendly. I figured I'd better get out of there before Alvin broke me in two. So, ready to head back?"

Chapter 6

Dad served one of his lumberjack breakfasts. After thirds, Dick leaned back and sighed. "I'm ready for a nap."

"You can take one in the boat," I said. "I thought we could motor up to Drowned Man Slough and float down. That's if you're not going to use the boat, Dad."

Dad lit a cigarette and reached for the coffeepot. "No, I'm just going to putter until Ned gets here. You boys go and have a good time."

In the boat, we headed back upstream, taking it easy this time. "Darn," Dick said, "I sure wish that Crystal and Sonia could have stayed." He gave me a crooked smile. "But it looks like you've got something going."

I snorted. "Izzy's just thirteen, remember? But she's a good kid."

"Uh-huh," he said. "Well, don't get in trouble for that, you know, statutatory rape thing."

"Statutory. And I'm underage, too. So, I'm not sure it'd count."

"They'd figure out a way to make it count, bubba. Start messing with a thirteen-year-old, and the law will definitely put a hurt on you."

"Well, no worries on that," I said. "She's just a friend."

We fished the west side of the river on the way upstream to Drowned Man Slough and then started floating down on the east side. By then we had a couple of pretty nice walleyes on the stringer. "I'm hungry," Dick said.

"The way you ate this morning, I didn't think you'd ever be hungry again."

"Well, I am. I wish we'd packed some sandwiches."

"We've got walleye."

"True. And you're itching to use that survival kit of yours, aren't you."

"You got it. Let's pull in over there. There's a campsite and a fire ring in that clump of pines."

While Dick gathered sticks and got a small fire going, I cleaned the fish. It's fairly simple to roast marshmallows or hot dogs on a stick, but fish fillets are a little tougher. But if you don't mind an ash coating and a few scorched fingers, they're pretty good.

Dick licked his fingers when he'd swallowed the last bite of his walleye. "That was good. . . . I bet Sonia and Crystal would have been really impressed with our woodsy skills."

"I don't think they would have cared much for ashes on their fish."

"Well, maybe not. Good idea having salt in your survival kit. That made them taste a lot better. And the ash isn't bad. Kind of gives them a smoky taste." He gazed out over the river. "You know, I could live up here."

"Me too. Someday I'm going to."

Dick slapped at a mosquito. "But I could do without the skeets."

"More skeets, fewer tourists."

"I suppose. Let's go before they eat us."

I got up and unzipped my fly. "Help me put out the fire."

"By pissing on it?"

"Yep, Bern calls it the Indian method. It works, and it's fun, too."

The sun was brushing the treetops on the west side of the river by the time we tied up to the dock at the lodge.

Walking up the hill, I heard Ned's short, harsh laugh. "Well, the jerk made it here," I said.

"You think Ned's a jerk?" Dick asked.

"Don't you?"

"Oh, I don't know. The couple of times I've met him he seemed like an okay guy."

I grunted, not wanting to argue about it.

Dad and Ned were sitting on the front porch with beers, shot glasses, and a fifth of scotch between them. "There they are," Ned said.

Dick and I shook hands with him. "Want a Coke?" I asked Dick.

"I'd rather have a beer, if that's okay with you, Mr. C."

"It's okay with me, Dick," Dad said. "Might as well bring us each one."

I brought four beers and sat with a bottle warming in my hand while the other three talked about fishing.

"So," Dad said, "Ned and I were thinking about going into town for supper. What do you boys want to do? There's lots of food in the refrigerator if you'd rather stay here."

"Going into town sounds good to me," Dick said. "What do you think, Andy?"

I was stuck. "I guess that would be okay."

We ate at the Pinery, one of those low-light, classy places with really boring elevator music. Dad and Ned led off with martinis, Dick and I with Cokes. The waitress brought our salads and a basket of crackers and then turned to clear off a table next to us. She was a big woman, and when she leaned over, Ned made as if to slap her broad butt. A woman at another table saw him and laughed. Ned didn't crack a smile. Instead, he turned his hand palm-up and made like he was going to pat the waitress up between her fat thighs. The woman at the other table turned away, blushing. Dad and Dick laughed, but I felt bad for the fat waitress and the woman Ned had embarrassed.

Dick and I finished our steaks first. "Let's go look for some action," Dick whispered.

"As in?"

"You know. Girls."

"You boys go have fun," Dad said. "You've got time to catch the movie at the theater, if you want to. We'll see you when you get back."

Out on the street, I snapped at Dick. "Damn it, I don't want to stay in town all night."

"Why not?"

"It's Sunday. Nothing's going on. And those two

will be really hammered if they sit there and drink for a couple of hours."

"Well, they'd drink back at the lodge or at Cattail's, wouldn't they?"

"Yeah, but then we wouldn't have to risk getting killed between here and there."

He shrugged. "You worry too much. They'll be fine. Come on. Let's see how this town parties."

It didn't. Or at least not on a Sunday night. We'd both seen the movie, so we ended up at the city park watching a softball game. Dick spent most of his time flirting with some girls, asking them all sorts of questions and getting mostly giggles in reply. As usual, I didn't have much to say.

Dick couldn't get the girls to hang around with us when the game wound up, so we wandered back down to the main drag and finally back to the Pinery. Dad and Ned were at the bar, watching a Brewers game on the TV. "Hi, boys," Dad said. "Make any time with the northern girls?" They both smirked.

"I tell you, Mr. C.," Dick said. "It was embarrassing. They were fighting over us, especially Andy. When they started going at each other with axes and stuff, we decided we'd better head back here."

They laughed.

Dad was walking okay when we got out on the street, and he seemed to drive okay, too. But we weren't five miles out of town when he pulled into the first bar. "Better check out the Cant-Hook," he said.

We trooped in. The two of them settled at the bar, ordering beers and shots. The pool table was open, and Dick shoved in some quarters. As usual, he cleaned my clock.

The table was open at the next bar, too, and I was behind five games to zip when we pulled in at the Bear Hound, ten miles from the lodge. By that time I had a headache from breathing cigarette smoke, and Dad wasn't walking so steady anymore. Ned didn't show that he'd had so much as a drink, and Dick, of course, was still hoping for some unattached girls. Some guys already had a pool game going and a sign on the electronic dart game said Out of Order, so there wasn't anything to do but wait around while Dad and Ned had a couple more shots and beer chasers.

I hoped Ned would drive the rest of the way, but this was a macho thing, and Dad climbed behind the wheel again. After an initial lurch and a wide turn coming out of the parking lot, he seemed fine. I relaxed a little, rolled down my window, and watched the night pass. The breeze brought in the smells of woods, swamp, and river and the sounds of crickets and bullfrogs. All peaceful, which made the swerve and the screech of tires all the scarier. We hit the left ditch, skidded along the slippery side, tilted left onto two wheels, slammed down on all four, and slid to a stop just short of a nosedive down the steep bank of one of those nameless creeks that leak out of the pine swamps and into the river. The car shuddered and stalled.

"Is everybody all right?" Ned demanded.

"I'm okay," I said.

"Me too," Dick said, his voice shaky.

"Oz, you okay?" Ned asked.

"Yeah. Yeah, I'm okay." Dad got a cigarette going with shaking fingers.

Ned swung his door open and the rest of us followed. There was surprisingly little damage. Probably some scrapes in the paint that would show up in daylight, maybe some damage to the undercarriage, but otherwise we seemed to have come out with only a broken grill.

Dick leaned close to me and whispered, "What happened?"

"I don't know. Maybe he just dozed off for a second."

Ned finished peering under the car with a flashlight. "Well, I think the car's okay. But we're going to need somebody to pull us out of the ditch."

Dad nodded. He hadn't said anything since getting

out of the car. "I . . . I thought I saw a deer coming out of the ditch on the right."

"Yeah," Ned said. "Maybe he turned back when you swerved. Let's you and me talk for a second."

Dad followed him up to the road, where Ned started talking low and emphatically. Dad nodded, staring at his shoes.

"Wow!" Dick said. "For a second I thought we were going to die."

"Me too. It would have been a lot worse if we'd gone over the bank and into that creek."

"Uh-huh." He wiped at his eyes, and I was surprised to see that his hands were shaking.

"Come on, Dick," Ned called. "We're going to walk down to Cattail's and see if we can get a tow."

They left. I joined Dad on the shoulder. "You okay?" I asked.

Dad didn't reply for a second. "I'm sorry, Andy."

"It's okay, Dad. Nobody got hurt, and there isn't much damage to the car."

He took a breath. "If a sheriff's deputy or state patrol car comes by, Ned thinks it would be better if you said you were driving. He took Dick with him so you can tell the officer it was just the two of us in the car."

I stared at him in amazement. "But, Dad, I don't want a record before I even have a license!"

"You'll probably just get a warning. Just tell him about the deer."

"I didn't see a deer."

"I did." He waved an arm at the opposite ditch. "It was coming out of that ditch over there." He didn't meet my eyes.

I didn't say anything.

He shrugged. "It's up to you."

Yeah, it was up to me. Take the hit for Dad or let him get a DUI. I took a breath, feeling that I was about to lose something I'd never get back. "Okay," I said. "If a cop comes by, I'll say I was driving."

"Even if one doesn't come by, that's probably still the best story for us to tell."

"You mean down at Cattail's?"

"And to Rodge and Bern."

So you don't look foolish, I thought. Let me have that pleasure. "All right," I said. I scrambled back down to the car, and leaned in the driver's door to turn off the headlights and the ignition. Might as well save the battery, if nothing else.

It's a lonely road, especially on a Sunday night after the tourists have headed home. A couple of drivers stopped to see if we needed help. I told them help was already coming and thanked them. Finally, Cattail came up the road in his big four-wheel-drive Dodge and pulled to a stop beside us. Izzy hopped down from the passenger seat. "Are you okay?" she asked me.

"Yeah. Fine."

"I was really worried when Dick and that big guy came in. Cattail and the big guy went out to the kitchen to talk. I asked Dick what had happened, and he said you'd gone off the road trying to miss a deer."

"Something like that," I said.

"But what's the big secret?"

"I'm not supposed to have passengers in the car with just a learner's permit."

"Oh."

Cattail had lined up so that he could winch us out backward. I took the hook and walked the cable down as Cattail unwound it from the drum. I got down on my hands and knees and looked under the car for a place to hook onto the frame. Izzy knelt beside me, shining a flashlight underneath. "Thanks," I said.

"No problem."

I found a good spot and hooked on. "Tell him to take up the slack."

She got up and waved the flashlight. The winch whined and the cable pulled tight. I scrambled out and went to the driver's door. "You'd better wait up on the highway," I said.

"I could sit beside you and help watch for stuff."

"Better not. In case somebody comes by."

I got the car started. "Just put it in neutral," Cattail called. "Let the winch do the work."

I swiveled so that I could look through the rear window. With a bump, the car started moving. I steered with my left hand, following the cable up to the road. The grade got pretty steep and I could hear the truck's engine laboring. Then the back wheels bumped over onto the shoulder and we came smoothly the rest of the way. I let out my breath, turned off the car, and scrambled out.

A few more minutes to unhook, wind up the cable, and get going, and we would have been okay. But then headlights came over the hill to the east and down toward us. When the car slowed and swung in behind Cattail's truck, I knew it was a cop. His light bar came on, illuminating us in flashing red and blue. A sheriff's deputy got out, settled his hat on his head, and came over to Cattail at the winch. "Hey, Cattail."

"Deputy Bob. How you doin'?"

"Good. Who was driving?"

"The boy over there. Good kid."

The deputy came over. He shined the flashlight in my face for a moment. "May I see your driver's license, sir."

I dug for my wallet. "I've just got my permit." I handed it to him.

"Who was with you?"

"Just my dad." I gestured to where Dad stood a few feet away.

"Here I am, officer," Dad said cheerily. "And here's my license."

The deputy studied my permit and then Dad's license under his flashlight. "Just a minute."

He went back to his car and sat behind the wheel. I could see him talking on the radio. Dad came over to stand with me. "You're doing fine," he said.

I could smell cinnamon on his breath and knew he was chewing gum furiously to cover the smell of booze. "Maybe you should go talk to Cattail," I said.

Dad slapped me on the shoulder and went over to Cattail, who had just finished running the cable back on the drum.

The deputy came back. "So, what happened?"

"A deer started coming across the road and I swerved to miss it."

"You know it's better to hit the deer than have an accident."

"Yeah, I know. But it had never happened to me before. I guess I kind of overreacted."

He grunted and looked at my permit again. "Had anything to drink tonight?"

"No, sir. Except Coke."

"Any pills, weed, anything that would show up if I took you in for a blood draw."

"No, sir. I don't do that stuff."

"Uh-huh. . . . Well, no damage done, so I'm just going to give you a warning. But you need to take it easy and keep your eyes open. There are a lot of deer in the woods."

"Yes, sir."

He took a ticket book out of his back pocket and started writing the warning. Done, he handed it to me along with my permit. "You take care, now."

"Yes, sir."

He stopped by Dad, Cattail, and Izzy to give Dad's license back to him. They talked for a couple of minutes. Then the three men laughed. They shook hands and the deputy sauntered back to his car. He pulled out, flipping off the light bar and giving us a wave as he passed.

I drove, following Cattail's pickup. "What did you pay Cattail?" I asked.

"Fifty bucks. Don't worry about it."

Believe me, I won't. "What were you guys laughing with the cop about?"

"Oh, he just said that his kids weren't teenagers yet but that he'd have to prepare himself for evenings like this."

"Ha, ha. Funny joke."

"Oh, you'll understand when you're a parent."

When we parked in front of Cattail's, I hoped Dick and Ned would come out right away. But Dad hopped out of his side and hurried in, leaving me to catch up. By the time I got inside, he was bellied up to the bar, laughing with Alvin Anderssen and Ned while Cattail got them all beers and shots. Dick came out and the two of us crossed the street and sat on the swings.

"I wish the girls were here," Dick said.

"Give it a rest, huh?"

"Well, they'd take our minds off things."

"Yours maybe."

Izzy came out of Cattail's house next to the tavern. "I'll go sit on a picnic table over there," Dick said.

"No need," I said.

"That's okay. I don't feel like talking anyway."

Izzy trotted across the road. "I can just stay out a few minutes. So, are you really okay?"

"Yeah, I guess."

"So what happened? You were driving, and—"

"No. Dad was driving. I just said I was so he wouldn't get a ticket for drunk driving."

"But Dick and that big guy said . . ." She let her voice trail off. I kicked at the earth worn bare of grass beneath the swing, afraid I might start crying if I met her eyes. "I guess they were lying, huh?" she said.

"Yeah," I said. "Everybody lied. . . . Doesn't that suck? My dad puts his car in the ditch and then asks me to take the blame."

"Did the cop give you a ticket?"

"Just a warning. But it'll be somewhere on my record."

"I'm sorry."

"Yeah, me too."

After she went in, Dick and I sat without talking until Dad and Ned came out half an hour later. At least Dad was smart enough to let Ned drive home.

Chapter 7

Dick was standing by the door, looking out on the morning, when I opened my eyes. His bed was made and his duffle stood packed beside it. "Hey, what's up, man?" I asked.

He stubbed out the cigarette he was smoking. "I guess I'm going back to Brunswick. I'm sorry, dude, but I'm just not comfortable being around here right now."

For a minute I couldn't think of anything to say. "I'm sorry about last night," I managed. "But things will get better today. I thought we could take the boat—"

"I already called my mom. She's gonna be here in a couple of hours."

"Well, call her back. Maybe she hasn't left yet."

He shook his head. "Nah, I don't think so, man. That stuff last night was pretty scary."

"What did you tell your mom?"

"That I wasn't feeling good. Don't worry. I won't tell her what happened." He lit another cigarette and stood smoking in the patch of sun coming through the door.

"Let's get some breakfast. Then we can talk about it."

"No, I don't want to go over there again. Sneaking in to use the phone was bad enough."

"I'll go get us some."

"Okay."

We ate on the picnic table in the backyard. "Dick, just give it a day," I said. "I'll talk to him. Ask him if they can cool it."

Dick looked up, meeting my eyes for the first time since he'd told me that he was going back to Brunswick. He shook his head slowly. "I've got an uncle with a drinking problem, and it's not something he can turn on and off. When Uncle Harlan drinks, that's what he does until something big happens. Like he gets arrested or his wife leaves him or he ends up in the hospital. That's the way it is for him, and I think your dad's kinda the same way."

I tried to keep the desperation out of my voice. "Oh,

Dad's not that bad. He just likes to cut loose a bit when he's up north, that's all."

Dick studied me for a moment. Then he shrugged. "Well, you know him better than I do."

Irrationally, I wanted to protect Dad, to lie for him. But Dick knew me and he knew Dad far too well to be fooled by anything I said.

"I gotta go, man," he said.

"I'll walk with you to the highway bridge. Just let me get my rod."

He glanced at the house. "That's okay. I think your dad's up now."

"He won't miss me." I put our cereal dishes in the kitchen sink and ran for my rod. I could hear Dad moving around in the master bedroom.

We traded off carrying Dick's duffle bag until we reached the highway. Dick glanced at the sky, which was turning a paler shade of blue as the day warmed. "It's going to be hot," he said.

"Yeah," I said, "but the fishing should be okay along the shady side of the river."

We fished from the highway bridge, the occasional car passing. "Mom should be here pretty soon," Dick said. "It's been nearly three hours."

"Is she really going to believe that you're not feeling good?"

He shrugged. "I'll tell her that I'm feeling better now. You know, ate something that didn't agree with me last night."

"Just as long as you don't tell her . . . well, you know my dad's a professional person and—"

"I know. Don't worry."

His mom's minivan came around the long curve from the west. She tapped the horn and waved. I helped Dick get his stuff into the back. We shook hands. "Sorry you have to go," I said.

"Yeah, me too. I'll see you when you get back to town." He looked down at his feet. "Don't let this stuff with your dad get you all screwed up again. It ain't worth that."

"I know," I said. "Don't worry. I'm past all that now."

When they'd gone, I trudged back to the town road and started up the long hill that never seems half as steep when you're in a car. Somewhere on the climb the Gloom started falling around me. By the time I was halfway up the hill, I was pausing every dozen steps to rest. To start again took a tremendous effort. Finally, I just sat down on the bank by the road and let the Gloom fall.

The Gloom always comes on me the same way. One minute everything is bright and warm and the next minute a cloud covers the sun, draining all the color out of the world, leaving everything gray. The birds quit singing and the squirrels stop chattering. People speak to me, but their voices are muffled, every other word too distorted to make out. And I know I'm fading to gray just like the colors, dulling out and going away.

The Gloom has been coming every few months for a long time now. Sometimes it'll just pass through like a fast-moving shower. Other times it will linger for weeks. Last summer, I didn't think the sun was ever going to shine again. I'm not exactly sure when the Gloom first visited, but it really got bad the fall Dad nearly crushed my legs against the garage door. That next morning Mom gave him an ultimatum: Come home sober or don't come home. I think he tried for a few days, but a week or so later something must have tipped her off that he was drinking.

When I got home from school that afternoon, she told me to do my homework on the front porch so that I could call her when the Ford turned our corner. "But I was going to play football with some of the guys," I said.

"I want you here this afternoon. This is more important."

"Why can't Rodge do it?"

"Rodge is with Bethany."

I could have whined about it, but her tone was

enough to warn me that she was already on the edge of losing her temper. I went.

Sylvia had her stuffed animals lined up in rows in the living room and was playing school. "Aren't you getting kind of old to be playing with stuffed animals?" I said.

She stared at me levelly, as if weighing whether I was worth half a dozen words or not. "I'm practicing being a teacher. Not playing."

So much for that discussion. I went out on the porch.

I made a halfhearted attempt at my social studies homework, but mostly I looked out the window until the Ford turned the corner an hour later. "He's coming, Mom," I called.

She strode in. "Come along, children."

"Why?" I said, although I was already moving.

"Because I want him to see what he's risking."

Sylvia and I trooped after her.

We stood on the walk at the top of the stone steps leading up from the driveway. Mom took Sylvia's hand and reached for mine. I edged away.

Dad pulled in, parked, and shut off the car. I could see him moving very deliberately, trying to cover up how much he'd had to drink. But he stumbled getting out of the car, and Mom let him have it full volume. She's forever telling us to mind what the neighbors think, but when she's really steamed, she'll just let 'er rip, neighbors be damned.

"I warned you, Oscar! So just get back in that car and get out of here!"

"Honey—"

"No, Oscar! I could tell before you even got out. You're drunk!"

"I just had a couple—"

"You are drunk! You are an alcoholic, Oscar. You can't drink at all. Now go on, leave! Leave your beautiful house and your beautiful children and your wife of twenty years. And don't come back until you're well!"

He went, and Mom marched us back inside.

In the living room, I turned on the TV. Sylvia sat down cross-legged on the floor and tapped a pencil on the book in front of her. "Now, children, pay attention. It's schooltime now."

After a few minutes, I went to the kitchen. Mom was at the stove, a dish towel over her shoulder. She didn't turn around. "Are you okay?" I asked.

She nodded, using a corner of the dishtowel to wipe her eyes. I stood there, trying to think of something to say. Finally, I went to my room and sat in front of my littered desk doing nothing. When I heard Rodge go into his room, I went to see him. He was at his desk already, his algebra book open in front of him. "Dad left," I said.

"I heard."

"Do you know where he went?"

"Nope."

"What are we going to do?"

"I don't know what you're going to do, but I'm going to study. Don't let the door hit you in the ass on your way out."

Dad drove all the way to his mother's in Baraboo. Grandma took him in and probably had a couple of drinks with him while he told her how no one loved him at home. I doubt that she argued much. Grandma's never liked Mom, and I don't think she particularly cares for her grandkids either. But at least she called Mom to tell her Dad was safe.

A couple of days later, Dad got arrested for chasing some kids off the lawn while dressed only in his boxer shorts. Grandma called Mom, and Mom drove down to Baraboo. She got the charges dropped on the condition that he go to the mental hospital at Winnebago for treatment. The hospital let him out just before Christmas, and Mom and Rodge went down to pick him and his car up. Sylvia and I stayed home. We ate TV dinners, cleaned up the kitchen, and then she went off to play with her stuffed animals, and I sat down to try to do homework. But I'm not like Rodge. So, I just sat at my desk, listening to the wind wrapping itself around our house like some big, sad animal.

They got home about nine, and we went down to the garage to greet them. Dad got out of Mom's car with his extra clothes in a shopping bag. He looked thinner and older, and his voice wasn't much more than a whisper when he said, "Hi, kids."

Maybe I should have run to him and given him a hug. But it was too weird having him back. Sylvia edged close to me. "Hi, Dad," I said. "How are you feeling?"

"Okay," he said.

Mom took his arm. "Come inside, Oscar. You can sleep in your own bed tonight."

Mom tried to make Christmas a success. We put up a tree, played Christmas carols, baked cookies, and did all that good stuff. But Dad just didn't seem interested. Somewhere in the days between Christmas and New Year's it became my job to sit with him. He had the shakes and couldn't sleep more than an hour or two at night without waking up in a sweat. I suppose he had nightmares, too. I know I did. Mom lost a lot of sleep, and somebody had to take over now and then so that she could rest. I got the job by default since Sylvia was too little and Rodge was with his girlfriend or his buddies most of the time.

New Year's Eve I lay beside Dad on his bed, reading to him from a book about the famous portage at Sault Ste. Marie and the great locks that were built there to connect Lake Superior to the lower lakes, the St. Lawrence River, and the sea. He chain-smoked, his hands shaking so hard that he could barely get the cigarettes lit. At midnight we heard firecrackers and car horns welcoming the New Year. Dad reached over to snap off the bedside lamp. We lay together in the dark, listening to the merriment on the night streets. "Happy goddamn New Year," he said bitterly.

"But we had fun, Dad," I said. "It's a good book."

He didn't reply to that, just lay staring at the lights reflecting on the ceiling from the cars passing on the street. "Don't ever let a woman tell you that you can't drink, Andy. It isn't right. A man needs to be with his friends on New Year's Eve."

I didn't reply, just curled up a little tighter. After a few minutes, he found the light again, managed to get a cigarette lit, and picked up his wallet. He handed me a five-dollar bill. "Here's for reading so well. You'd better get to bed now. Close the door behind you."

In my room, I sat staring at the cover of *The Mighty Soo* with its stories of Indians, fur traders, engineers, and sailors. I've still got that book. On the cover is a picture of a big ore boat emerging from the locks into Lake Superior. I love that picture. Someday I'd like to stand on the highest point of one of those boats with the breeze in my face and the morning sun on my shoulders, watching the gates swinging wide and the big lake spreading open ahead, clear and blue all the way to the horizon.

I'd been sitting by the road for half an hour maybe, my thoughts crawling like maggots on the body of a dead dog, when I heard a voice: "Are you okay?"

I looked up, my eyes taking a moment to focus on the girl standing by a bicycle. Izzy. "Yeah, I'm okay."

"You don't look okay."

"I'm okay. What are you doing here?"

"Exploring. What are you doing here?"

"Nothing much. Just thinking."

"Are you feeling sick?"

"No, I'm okay."

"You could ride my bike. I don't mind walking."

"Thanks, but that's okay. Where are you going?"

"We only had a couple of cabins to clean, so I got off early. I decided to see where this old road goes."

"It dead-ends about three miles from here. It used to run all the way to County Q near White Buck tavern, but not since they logged off most of the pulp down in the state forest."

"Isn't a road a road? Why can't you get through now?"

"A lot of trees blown down, bridges out, brush growing over the road. My brother's friend Bern and I tried to get through a couple of summers ago on a four-wheeler. It's impossible."

"You've got a four-wheeler?"

"No. Bern did. He sold it."

"Darn. I'd like to go four-wheeling."

"If I ever get one, I'll take you."

"Well, if you're all right, I guess I'll get going."

"Okay. I'll see you later."

"Thanks for the warning." She hopped onto her bike and peddled up the hill, the wheels bumping over the rocks and ruts.

For the few minutes I'd talked to her the world had seemed bright again, but the Gloom wasn't going to let go that easily. By the time I started down the driveway to the lodge, it was back big-time, and I wasn't so much walking as creeping from shadow to shadow. I couldn't let Dad and Ned see me like this. If I took a little more time by myself, maybe the Gloom would drift away.

I left the road and circled through the woods until I reached the downstream side of the lodge. I paused a minute to listen and then scuttled across to the porch and slithered underneath.

The lodge was built on thick concrete posts seventy or eighty years ago. The outer logs are low to the ground but the crawl space under the floor is almost three feet high. The rain and the snow only get in around the edges, leaving the rest dry and smelling of earth and ancient decay. When I was a kid, I was scared of the crawl space and used to imagine monsters lurking beneath the lodge. But a couple of summers ago I discovered what a neat place it was to hide. I could crawl under the lodge and hide for hours while the sounds of life went on above me. I was safe under the lodge, out of sight and out of mind. When I heard Mom or Dad start asking where I was, I could crawl out and walk innocently back into the world.

Mom caught me at it early last summer. She was pissed big-time and accused me of eavesdropping. She made me promise not to go under the lodge again. But a few days later, Dad got really drunk and threatened Mom and then me, and I couldn't deal with it anymore. So I crawled under the lodge, curled up, and just kind of checked out of everything. I was under there a long time before they found me. Rodge and Bern had to crawl in to pull me out by the ankles.

I don't remember much more of that afternoon. Hell, I don't remember much more of that week. I know I was in a car for a long time and then in a white place with cool white sheets and there were people trying to talk to me and shots and a tube in my arm that I tore out and that they put back in, telling me that I had to be a good boy. And I slept hours and hours, whole days it seemed, not caring to do anything but curl up and sleep some more. I woke in another place, and there were new people trying to talk to me and then hands that bathed me and gently uncurled me and kept uncurling me until I started waking up and trying to make out what people said.

I learned a new word: *catatonia,* which struck me as not such a bad word, a word that might describe a cat curling up, warm and safe, and just not giving a damn about doing anything but sleep. And thinking about that old cat, I would just as soon have gone back to sleep and done the catatonia thing forever, except that people kept saying I couldn't, that I had to sit up, eat, listen, and learn to deal with all sorts of shit that I had no interest in dealing with but that they wouldn't stop talking about.

When I started coming out of it, they gave me pills, and kept talking to me and trying to get me to talk.

Sometimes it was just me and a doctor or a social worker or somebody with some other title. Other times, I had to attend group therapy, where a bunch of other screwed-up kids were supposed to talk everything out and get well together. I hated group.

Every once in a while, somebody on the ward would really lose it, and nurses and attendants would come running and wheel the kid away on a gurney, a shot in his arm and wrapped so tight in a sheet that he couldn't move. We wouldn't see that kid for two or three days and then he would be a lot quieter, his eyes dull and unfocused. I made up my mind that I wasn't going to let that happen to me, and stuck with that until the day I tried to kill a couple of snotty bastards in group.

They finally let me out of the hospital after a month with a lot of head meds and a couple of pretty major holes in my memory from the time after I'd lost it in group and gone after those guys. I went up to the lodge only one more time that summer, and Mom made me promise that I'd never hide in the crawl space again. And I hadn't. Not until the Gloom fell out of the sky on me while I was climbing that long, dusty hill after my best friend left and a girl named Izzy asked if I was okay and I'd lied and told her that I was when I wasn't and hadn't been for a long time. Maybe never.

Squeezing under the outside log was a little like

coming back to the place I belonged. I paused to catch my breath and then crawled over the dry earth until I reached the big white pine stump beneath the door from the main room to the porch. The lumberjacks who'd built the lodge had cut big pine and hemlock trees to make a clearing in the woods. They didn't pull the stumps, but cut them low to the ground and built over the top of them. As the years passed, the ground sank, exposing a web of dry roots around the stumps. I could dig down in the powdery soil with my fingers and wrap my hands around roots as thick as a forearm. Tug and I could feel them running deep in the ground, still holding though the tree above had crashed to earth long ago. When I'm dead, I want to be like one of those roots. I don't want to fly free of earth, don't want to rise up into blue sky. I just want to hold on to the earth in some dry, secret place, where I never have to think again, but only sleep.

Voices on the porch woke me. Dad and Ned were eating a late breakfast from the sound of things. Dusty whined and Dad said, "Here you go, boy. Lick it clean, and we won't have to wash it."

Ned belched. "Great food, Oz. You're a hell of a cook."

"Sure you've had enough? I thought Dick and Andy would be joining us, so there's plenty left."

"I'm full, and they'll be hungry when they get back. They got going plenty early."

"Well, Dick's a go-getter. He must have rousted Andy out so they could get a line in the water not long after the sun came up."

"Yeah, the Hammond boy is a good kid."

"He's good for Andy. I never mind it when he comes up here. Takes a lot of the worry off my shoulders."

"How's Andy been doing?"

Dad sighed. "Better, I guess. But he's still in his own little world most of the time. Rodge and Bern have been real patient, but it's hard for them to get much work out of him. He'd rather be off in the woods by himself."

"But you say he doesn't hunt?"

"No. He used to love shooting at cans at the dump. But a couple of years ago he shot a chipmunk. That really bothered him."

"He got upset over a chipmunk?"

Dad snorted. "Yeah. I shot my first deer when I was twelve, but Andy couldn't stop crying about a chipmunk."

Ned made a sound of disgust. "There are a lot of chipmunks in the world, a fair number of them in the stomachs of owls and foxes."

"That doesn't seem to bother him. This spring we surprised a fox with a couple of baby rabbits in his mouth. And Andy didn't bat an eye at that. Even said he was glad the fox would have a good supper."

"So he's only sentimental about chipmunks?"

"I guess. I've tried to talk to him rationally about it, but he just clams up. Most of the time he's pretty shy about talking to adults, even me."

"Well, he sure wasn't shy telling me off about the Brewers the last time I was up here."

Dad sighed again. "I know, Ned. I'm sorry he gave you that crap. He was wrong, and I think he knew it."

"It's okay, Oz. I know you work hard as hell with him. He'll come around."

"God, I hope so. His therapist told us that he thought Andy could hold his own over the summer. When school starts, we'll get him in for a few sessions, just to make sure he's headed the right way."

"This therapist have any new ideas about the problem?"

"Not really. Pretty much goes along with the diagnosis the hospital made: nonspecific anxiety coupled with moderate depression. Hell, I could have told them that."

"And he's got medications?"

"Oh, yeah. Pills for anxiety, depression, and delusions."

"Delusions? Does he think he's Napoleon or something?"

Dad laughed. "Not that he's told me. I guess it's . . . I don't know. Feeling that people gang up on him. Or that his mom and I love Rodge more than him. Or that chipmunks have feelings. More along that line."

"How were his grades last spring?"

"Terrible. His mother would have put him in summer school, but I told her he'd be better off spending the summer up here with Rodge and Bern. The psychologist agreed with me on that one, anyway."

"How's she dealing with his problems these days?"

"Well, I wish she had more patience. Half the time she's yelling at him and trying to rev him up, the rest of the time she's blaming herself for not raising the perfect child. She got it in her head that she ought to take him out East when her dad had heart surgery, but I talked her out of it. Hell, he would have gone nuts being cooped up with the old folks. I wouldn't have blamed him either."

I heard ice clink in a glass. "So," Ned said, "shall I mix us one more for the road?"

"Sounds good. I'll start cleaning up."

"So, you really think that title search missed something, huh?"

"Something doesn't add up. With a couple of hours to dig in the records, I think we'll find whatever it is. I'd bet money that title isn't clear."

I could hear Dad taking the dirty dishes to the

kitchen while Ned mixed the drinks. When they started talking again, it was about the court case, and I faded out. Eventually, they'd find me. Or Rodge and Bern would when they got back. And if no one ever did, that was fine with me.

I'm not sure when they left. I slept into the hot afternoon, lying flat on my belly, the dry earth against my cheek. I was slimy with sweat, the air around me stifling when I finally woke. For the first time in all the times I'd hidden under the lodge, I felt claustrophobic. I crawled out as fast as I could and swayed to my feet, still foggy with sleep and sweat. I filled my lungs with fresh air and became suddenly aware that something had changed. The world around me had colors again—colors and the sounds and the fragrances of the forest on a hot summer afternoon.

I stumbled down the hill to the river, stripped off my clothes, and plunged in, let the current take me as I sank to the dark bottom, and when I couldn't stay down any longer, I kicked upward, bursting into air as bright as autumn leaves. I swam for the shore, climbed out, and stood naked in the sunlight, letting the air dry me and knowing exactly what I had to do.

Dusty was asleep at the end of his chain in a patch of shade beneath a birch in the backyard. He lifted his head to gaze at me with mild curiosity. "Aren't you at least going to bark?" I asked. He wagged his tail twice and then laid his head back down and closed his eyes. God, what a great pal.

In the kitchen I slapped together two peanut butter sandwiches, stuck one in a baggie, and ate the other. A note and a pencil lay on the table: "Boys, Ned and I ran up to Longridge to do some research at the courthouse. Get a good meal. If you want to go to Cattail's for burgers, just tell him to charge it. We'll be back this evening."

I hesitated and then picked up the pencil stub and wrote: "Gone camping."

I filled my water bottle in the bathroom and dug around in the medicine cabinet until I found the bottle of water purification tablets that had stood there for years. I left behind my bottles of prescription pills. Screw the head meds. In the guest cabin, I changed into clean underwear, jeans, hiking shirt, and boots. I stuffed my Gore-Tex rain jacket into my belt pack along with a topographical map and the water bottle, buttoned an apple into one pocket of my shirt and the sandwich into the other, and then clipped my survival kit to my belt. And when I had all I needed, I headed into the woods with no plan except never coming back. That's it. I just walked away and kept walking.

One night late, I saw a movie set in the Australian out-back. A little aborigine girl with no family looks at a white woman who is her friend and announces matter-of-factly that she is "going walkabout." I liked that a lot—the whole idea of just setting out with no plan and no purpose except to see what lay beyond the next hill or horizon or mirage. Just going.

I didn't call what I was doing a *walkabout* because I wasn't in Australia and it didn't seem right somehow to steal the word. Besides, there was more purpose to what I was doing. I was leaving: going on a *walkaway*.

Last summer, when I'd crawled under the lodge, the Gloom had taken me away from it all. And when the doctors and the nurses and the head meds had made me come back, I'd come back with a lot of the Gloom still sticking to me. Today I'd come all the way around again, crawled back into the dimness under the lodge and let the heat and the stillness sweat the Gloom out of me. This time I'd crawled out on my own and was no longer crazy, or at least not crazy in the same way I'd been when I'd given a damn about the people yelling on the other side of the floor over my head. From now on, they could solve their own problems or not solve them. I no longer cared.

I crossed Balsam Creek at the ford I'd used on the day I'd rescued the crow and followed the same deer path to the river, where the narrow floodplain made for good walking. South half a mile I came to one of the nameless rivulets that drain into the river. It was nearly dry and so narrow that I could have jumped across and kept following the river, but I decided to see how far it ran inland. I kept to its winding course for the rest of the afternoon until it finally disappeared into a wide pine swamp. I'd tried to cross similar swamps in the past and knew it was nearly impossible before a hard freeze in the autumn. Bern said that some of these swamps had probably never been crossed by a man on foot in the summer. I didn't know if that was true, but I knew they were lonely places, inhabited in the months between thaw and freeze only by birds, muskrats, snakes, and a few other small, harmless creatures.

I climbed a low hill just high enough to catch a breeze to keep the bugs off. I stripped off my hiking shirt and let the breeze cool my sweaty T-shirt while I checked the map. I hadn't had it open all afternoon, but I wasn't far off from where I'd figured despite all the rivulet's twists and turns: two miles south and half a mile east of the lodge. Not a bad piece of woodcraft. Bern would have been proud of me. I stowed away the map, lay back on the mossy ground, and gazed off across the swamp. A crow flapped onto a maple branch and stared down at me. Could it be my crow? Not very likely, but at least it wasn't Poe's Raven grumbling about Nevermore, Lenore, and being *really* depressed. I waved. Nope, not carrion yet, dude. Try for some fish heads by the river or some roadkill on the highway.

The crow gave a disgusted caw and flapped off.

I dozed for an hour, waking to a sky already darkening to a deep blue. I felt a moment of panic then. I'd have to move fast to make the town road in daylight. Then I thought: Wait a second, you walked away, remember? You don't have to move from this spot if you don't want to. I checked my water bottle. A cup left, maybe a little more. I'd be thirsty in the morning, but I wasn't going to cross the Sahara between here and the nearest creek. I'd have to boil the water or give the purification tablets a couple of hours to work, but I'd be okay.

I gathered a pile of twigs and small sticks, and scraped out a fire ring. I dug down through to black soil with the lip of the Sierra cup, pushed the humus well out of the way so that I wouldn't confuse it with black dirt, and then dug down another few inches, piling the loose dirt to the side so that I could use it to smother the fire later. I took a lot of care constructing the fire, just as Bern had taught me, so I'd be sure to get it on the first match. It took me two, actually, but that wasn't bad.

I watched the fire while I ate my sandwich slowly, washing it down with sips of warm water. How long could I live out here by myself if I really tried? I could pick blueberries and raspberries, catch fish in the creeks, and forage for some of the edible plants I knew. As long as I didn't contract beaver fever from drinking bad water, I could last quite a while. Or at least a few days. Or until it rained or I ran out of bug dope.

I let my mind run on, imagining how I might do it. I even fantasized about running into a wild woods girl, perhaps raised by coyotes or something. She'd be wearing only an otter pelt around her waist, maybe some moccasins on her feet, and a flower in her long dark hair. Dick's voice broke in on my fantasy. "Now that babe is going to be even hairier than your buddy Tizzy."

"Izzy," I said. "And Izzy took a shower and shaved."

"So does your wild woods girl bathe?"

"Oh, sure," I said. "And she uses wintergreen for a deodorant."

"Why? Do the coyotes mind if she stinks?"

"She does. She's just naturally a clean girl."

"Except for the body hair."

"Forget about the body hair. You're hung up on that."

"Why hasn't this babe ever joined civilization?"

"Just figured it sucked from what she saw spying on

the deer hunters and fishermen. Besides, her coyote parents warned her about it."

"She speaks fluent coyote, I gather."

"Oh, yeah. Can talk to all the animals."

"You're nuts," he said.

"Maybe. But she sure is fun to imagine."

With my supper done, I started getting ready for some shut-eye. With a little more advance planning, I might have made a bed of leaves, but the soft moss wasn't bad. I cut out a square with the blade of my Leatherman for a pillow, reminding myself that I'd have to replace it in the morning. "Leave nothing but tracks," Bern preached, "and not even those if you can help it."

I put on another layer of bug dope and then unzipped and emptied my bladder on the fire. I kicked the black dirt over what was left, and stomped it down hard to smother the coals. Then I lay down to watch an orange moon rise over the swamp. I fell asleep happier than I'd been in a long time.

Chapter 8

I woke shivering in the first gray light. Some mosquitoes had gotten inside my collar and sucked out a pint or two of blood. And I was hungry. I replaced my moss pillow and cleaned up the site of my fire. With my head clearing, I had an odd, itchy sensation of someone or something watching me. I turned very slowly, a number of improbable but nasty possibilities coming to mind. The crow—or rather *a* crow—sat watching me from the top of a small spruce. We were only ten feet apart and just about at eye level in the gray light—which might have been kind of scary in an Attack-of-the-Vampire-Crows sort of way if he hadn't looked so comical. The spruce top was small and he was big and he bobbed up and down a good foot, like a crow on a trampoline. He didn't seem uncomfortable.

"Now, look," I said. "This kind of weirds me out. If you're the crow I saved from that trap, fine. You're welcome. Now stop sneaking up on me. If you're just any old crow looking for a meal, I'm not available. Not even close." I did a couple of jumping jacks. "See? Fit, able, and alive. No death in the near future. So shove off." He tilted his head, seemed to consider that. "Any questions?" I asked.

The top of the spruce bounced up and he gave a hop and was in the air and flapping away. He cawed. Which I suppose I could have taken any number of ways.

I made it to the town road as the sun came up over the trees. I jogged for a hundred yards to get warm and then settled into a walk to enjoy the birdsong and scent of pine on the morning breeze. I reached the old wooden bridge over Balsam Creek. I loved that bridge and was sorry to hear that the town was going to replace it with a big culvert. I found a dry stick and broke it into three roughly equal lengths for a quick game of Pooh sticks. I chose the piece I liked best and assigned the other two to Rodge and Sylvia. I dropped them on the upstream side of the bridge and hurried across to see which came out first. Rodge's did, followed by Sylvia's, and then—after a long delay—mine. Typical.

My stomach growled. Okay, I'll confess it. Hungry as I was right then, it didn't seem like such a bad idea to head back to the lodge. This early, I could raid the refrigerator and be back in the woods before anyone noticed. (Unless, of course, my half-witted dog took it into his head to bark.) Or, I could even make a bigger compromise and hang around to see if Dad was going to cook one of his lumberjack breakfasts. But what kind of wuss was I? This was my walkaway, damn it! That little aborigine girl went on her walkabout wearing nothing but a saggy dress with holes in it. I had a rain jacket, sturdy clothes, and good boots. She had nothing for equipment but a walking stick and a ratty foraging bag with maybe a little food in it. I had my survival kit, the Leatherman, and my water bottle. She was maybe eight or nine, I was almost sixteen. And she'd taken on the outback, for God's sake! I had a forest with streams to fish and plants to forage and civilization not more than a mile away. Bottom-line difference between us? She had a lot more guts. Okay. No going back. Not today, not tomorrow. Maybe never, or at least not until I was damned good and ready.

By the creek, I squatted and reached out as far as I could to fill my water bottle. In this country, creeks don't flow crystal clear like mountain brooks. Our creeks drain out of the land, carrying sediment and vegetable matter that give the water a brownish hue and an earthy aroma. The water tastes great, but you've got to boil it or treat it, or risk swallowing some really nasty bacteria and parasites. According to Bern, drinking giardia-contaminated water results in repeated attacks of green projectile diarrhea with an odor that can gag a buzzard. Unless you can get to the doctor for something to kill the parasites, you may crap yourself to death before your body can get the job done on its own. According to my foraging book, you can treat giardia with coptis or goldenseal, but I don't imagine it's a lot of fun foraging between bouts of projectile diarrhea. Personally, I'd rather be careful with the water. So instead of drinking, I crushed a purification tablet into the bottle of creek water, shook it a few times, and put it back in my belt pack.

I followed the creek upstream, heading for a spot Bern and I had found early last summer. We'd been fishing for trout and paused to eat our lunch in a grove of big hemlock trees by a shallow pool a few hundred feet above the bridge. The trees shaded out the brush so that the ground cover was mainly grass, moss, and needles. We'd commented then how nice a place it would be to camp, but we'd never done it.

The spot was a little brushier and buggier than I'd remembered and quite a bit closer to the road, but it was still a nice spot. I cut a green branch from an alder, rigged a fishing pole, and made myself comfortable. The morning light filtered through the trees, warming my back and patterning the water with reflections. The cricket I used for bait floated on the surface of the pond, minnows darting up to nudge and nibble at him. Finally, a shadow shot upward and the tip of my pole bent as a trout took the bait. I flicked the tip back to set the hook, felt the return pressure, and snapped the pole back to land the fish before he could run with the hook. Not artful, but it got the job done.

He was a pretty nice fish, eleven inches or a little better. By now I could have eaten three his size and a couple pounds of fries, but after another cricket and another hour, I decided the trout were done feeding for the morning. I got a fire going, gutted my fish, and roasted him over the flames. With a sprinkle of salt and a handful of the watercress from the edge of the stream, the trout made a pretty good first course. Problem: I didn't have a second course.

I still had a line in the water, my pole propped on a forked stick, a rock on the butt end, and a cricket drifting with the current. I'd put my fire out and was just about to get moving when a trout splashed and the tip of my pole bent. Well, thank you, big guy. Actually, not-so-big guy, but big enough to eat. I got him in and dispatched him with a crack on the head with a rock. I cleaned him, wrapped him in wet ferns, and buried him in the spongy, cool soil by the creek, where he'd keep for a few hours. Now for some salad to go with the trout.

Leaving my campsite, I actually looked around for the crow. I wasn't an expert in crow behavior, but I knew a few things: A flock is called "a murder of crows," which is kind of creepy. They can live for thirty years, although in a world with shotguns, great horned owls, and miscellaneous other ways to get reduced to a pile of black feathers, that isn't very likely. As birds go, they're smart as hell. You can actually teach a pet crow a few words. They clean up after predators, including automobiles. They like songbird eggs and chicks. They'll even follow a squirrel to its nest and have a few squirrelettes for supper. Would a crow also peck up a buried trout and gobble it down while the fisherman was wandering about in the woods foraging? If I came back and found the crow picking its beak with a fish bone, I was going to be pissed. I went back and stacked some rocks on my cache.

About twenty times that afternoon, I wished I'd brought my plant guide. I probably passed up a lot of edible stuff, but the first thing you learn about foraging is: Don't take chances! Since one cubic centimeter of a mushroom of the *amanita* family can kill you very dead, it's good advice to follow. I did manage to find fireweed, cowslip,

Indian salad, chickweed, bunchberries, and a few wild strawberries. In the course of the afternoon, I surprised a doe and a couple of fawns, stood still to let a skunk mosey past, and spent twenty minutes watching a wood-chuck mother and some of her half-grown kids digging up roots. And, of course, there were the usual squirrels, chipmunks, rabbits, garter snakes, toads, frogs, and birds, particularly crows for some reason.

When I figured I had enough for at least three meals, I folded my gatherings in my shirt, tying the sleeves and the tail together to make a bundle. Heading back to camp, I came upon a good patch of blackberries. I ate as many as I could and filled my cap.

I was back at my campsite by the middle of the afternoon. In the distance, when the wind was right, I could hear Rodge and Bern hammering on the roof of the garage. I could imagine Rodge bitching about how Dick and I had gone camping just to get out of doing any work. But I figured I had a day yet before anybody really got interested in tracking us. Dad and Ned would be up in Longridge most of the time and Rodge wouldn't exactly worry himself sick. Oh, they might be a little sur-prised when we didn't come back tonight. By noon tomorrow, they might start worrying, probably enough to start driving the roads to see if they could spot us. By

Thursday morning, projectile diarrhea would definitely be hitting the fan.

I took a siesta and then fished through the late afternoon. I landed a good trout this time and released half a dozen small ones. I gathered firewood for the evening and set about making supper. I boiled water in my Sierra cup and cooked down a good helping of the plants I'd foraged. That took more time than I'd figured, and it was dusk by the time I started roasting the two trout on a forked stick. Everything was about ready when I heard someone coming through the woods. He was moving quietly; not stealthily, just effortlessly, and I knew only one person who could move like that.

"Hey, Bern," I said.

"Hey, Andy. How you doin'?"

"Not bad. You're just in time for supper."

He sat down next to me and examined the pile of plants I'd picked. "Any wood hemlock in here?"

"Nope. I know better than that."

"Good. That stuff will flat-ass kill you." He plucked some of the cooked vegetables from my Sierra cup and chewed. "Not bad. Tastes sort of like spinach. Treating your water?"

"I'm doing everything you taught me. How are things back at the ranch?"

"Good. We came back last night to finish up the roof. Your dad and his partner went up to Longridge this morning for a meeting with a lawyer from the other side. They think they can get a settlement without going to court."

"I guess they found something at the courthouse yesterday."

"I guess so. They explained some of it last night, but I'm not clear on the details."

"Meaning that they were too smashed to make much sense."

"They'd had a few, but I wasn't real interested anyway."

"How'd things go in Storm Lake?"

He grinned. "Real good. I'm going back in a day or two to see if I can find some work."

"Rodge going?"

"Nah, I don't think so. Says he still has some work he wants to do on the lodge. . . . So, you headed back there after supper?"

"Hadn't planned on it."

"Well, Rodge is getting a little worried."

"I left a note."

"Yeah, but everybody thought Dick was with you."

"And everybody trusts Dick more than me."

Bern shrugged. "Well, you know, last summer and everything . . . Anyway, Dick called this afternoon to talk to you. That was the first we knew you were out here on your own. That got Rodge pretty shook up, especially when he looked and saw you hadn't taken your pills with you."

"I brought a few with me," I lied. "Tell him not to worry; I know what's good for me. So, did he call Dad's cell? There's service around Longridge, I think."

"He thought about it, but then said we ought to try to find you first. He went up to Cattail's to ask if anybody had seen you. I said I'd have a look around the neighborhood on my own. I remembered this spot and had a hunch that you might be down here."

"It's a good spot."

"Yeah, it is."

I took the fish off the fire, broke off one fork of the stick, and handed it to him. "Eat hearty."

"Thanks. Sure there's enough?"

"Yeah. I can always cook some more veggies."

"I've been meaning to try making a fry stick that would kind of pinch the fillets." He described what he had in mind.

"Yeah, I can see that. Maybe I'll try it tomorrow."

"So you're thinking of staying out for a while longer?"

"Why not? More fun than running gofer or watching Dad and Ned drink."

"Uh-huh . . . So why'd Dick go home, anyway?"

I told him about the accident. He winced. "Is that going on your record?"

"I suppose so. I wonder if the drivers' examiner will know about it when I take my test."

"You'll probably be okay." He didn't sound hopeful.

"Anyway, Dick left yesterday morning. Called up his mom and told her he wasn't feeling good. He told me he just wasn't comfortable around Dad and Ned anymore. I doubt if he'll ever come up here again. When I got back from walking Dick down to the highway, I heard Dad telling Ned about me going crazy last summer and what a loser I've always been. That was it for me. I grabbed a few things and headed out. Why not? I don't count for anything back there."

"I wouldn't say that."

"I would."

"Were you under the lodge when you heard them talking?"

"Yeah, I was."

Up to this point, Bern had been cool, but now his face twisted in genuine pain. "Doggone it, Andy. You know you shouldn't do that. Last summer, when Rodge and I went under to get you—"

"I came out on my own this time. This isn't like then. I'm not crazy now; I'm just pissed."

"So, what's the real deal, Andy?"

"I'm on strike."

"Why?"

"Because I'm sick of everybody. Except you and this girl I met the other day. You two I can still stand."

"Well, if I had a filly on my lasso, I wouldn't be down here in the woods."

"She's only thirteen. Just a friend."

He ate his last bite of fish and licked his fingers. "Good fish." He looked up at the patch of sky still visible above the trees. "I still think it'd be better if you came back to the lodge tonight."

"Sorry, no can do."

"You know, I've been hanging around your family for years. Your mom and dad have been real nice to me since my old man died. And Rodge is my best friend. I know he's hard on you sometimes, and I know your dad's got a drinking problem, but you guys have got the lodge, and your dad makes good—"

"Bern, I know all that. But I'm still not going back."

"You can't stay out here forever."

"Probably not, but I'm fine for right now. The survival kit works great."

He hesitated. "You really taking your pills?"

"Don't worry, I'm taking what I need."

"Well, think about coming back tonight, huh? We're supposed to get thunderstorms late."

"I'll think about it."

He nodded. "So, I'll see you later, maybe. Thanks for supper."

He moved off into the woods, walking like an Indian. I listened, trying to follow his movements. I liked Bern, but that didn't mean I trusted him. I heard gravel crunch as he climbed up the embankment to the road, and then I heard an electronic squawk and him talking. Shit! I'd forgotten the pair of small FRS radios in the dining room cabinet that Dad had bought when he thought he could make me into a deer hunter.

I kicked earth over the fire, jammed the loose stuff from my survival kit into my pockets, wadded up my jacket, and grabbed my water bottle and Sierra cup. I glanced around to make sure I hadn't forgotten anything and started for the woods. And stopped. Hell, I couldn't leave the fire smoldering under a little dirt! I dumped the contents of my water bottle on it, refilled it at the creek, dumped it again, and then filled and dumped it a third time. I heard a car coming on the road. I stamped on the sodden dirt to make doubly sure and ran for the woods.

I'm not Bern, and I can't move through the brush with hardly a sound. In a few feet I stopped trying to run and started moving with as much stealth as I could. I hadn't made it a hundred feet when I saw their flashlights and crouched down behind a tree.

Rodge swore. "Damn it! He took off."

"I was afraid of that," Bern said. "I told you we should have waited and given him a chance to come out on his own."

The beams of their flashlights probed the brush for me. "Andy, goddamn it!" Rodge yelled. "Just cut the crap and get your stupid ass back here."

"Damn it, Rodge!" Bern said. "That's not gonna do it."

For a second I couldn't make out what they were saying. But when Rodge shouted again, he was trying to sound reasonable. "Andy, look. I'm sorry you're pissed off about things. But hiding in the woods isn't going to solve anything. Just come back. We'll call Mom and talk to her. We'll work things out."

Like hell we will, I thought. Still crouching, I turned away, and slipped like a coyote into the brush. Above me feathers beat on air and I caught the brief silhouette of black wings outspread against a starry sky.

Chapter 9

Once I had my night vision, I could move pretty well. After a while, it seemed that every branch and bush, every fern and blade of grass took on a glow as if touched with a faint green luminescence. I was alone and not alone, the night breathing with the collective life of all the creatures sheltered in the forest. How many of them watched me, wondered in their animal way at the young human walking alone through their night world? Twice I thought I caught a glimpse of yellow eyes, and twice I heard the squeak and the scamper of a mouse or a vole getting out of my way. But mostly it was quiet except for the hum of insects, the croaking of frogs, and the far-off hooting of an owl. Still, I knew all the time I walked that he was with me, that if I chose to look over my left shoulder I would see him, black against starry blackness, following me on silent, ragged wings tinged with green fire.

By the time I stopped walking, lightning etched storm clouds against the western sky, and I could hear the first faint rumblings of thunder. I crawled under the drooping boughs of a Norway spruce, breaking off dead branches until I'd made a cave where I could stretch out. I wrapped myself in my jacket, cushioned my head on an arm, and watched the lightning flicker through gaps in the hanging boughs.

I didn't blame Bern for telling Rodge where I was. What else could he do? At least he'd come alone to see me first, and I appreciated that. It had been good to talk to someone. His question about the head meds had surprised me. I guess I'd assumed that everybody thought I was taking them. Truth was, I hadn't been taking them for nearly a month. The first couple of times, I'd just forgotten and hadn't felt any worse. So I thought: What the hell, let's see what happens. At first I flushed my daily dose down the toilet. But I stopped doing that after a while. Hell, nobody was counting or really cared as long as Andy was nice and calm and not causing any fuss.

I really didn't feel any worse without the pills. Matter of fact, I felt better. Nothing real major or specific. Just more awake, like I had an edge again after being dull for months. A couple of times when I got really down,

I'd taken an antidepressant. And I took an anti-anxiety pill a time or two when I was really worried about Dad. But I hadn't taken the one for delusions at all. I mean, what was with this delusions crap, anyway? I had fewer delusions than anyone in the family! And I should be taking pills that fuzzed up things and made me sleepy? Screw that.

I suppose the whole crow thing was just a little too weird to be true. But if the feeling that he was following me was a delusion, it wasn't much of one. If I thought I was being followed by a bloody-beaked pterodactyl, now that would be a delusion worth having. But a crow? Hell, it was hardly worth worrying about.

Anyway, I wasn't mad at Bern. He'd helped drag me out from under the lodge last summer, and I suppose that had scared him a lot more than he let on. And it had scared Rodge and the rest of them, too. Maybe it should have scared me more than it did. But I'd known for years that I was on the edge of going nuts. The real surprise was that I'd kept my balance as long as I had. That just happened to be the afternoon I finally lost it. A surprise, but not a big one.

Yeah, I'd scared the hell out of them all right, and I still scared them because the next time I went nuts might be worse—a whole lot worse. Did they sleep with their doors locked at night or with an eye open when there was no door between me and them? Did they worry that some night I'd take the rusty, double-bladed ax down from the wall of the garage and come to see them, each one in turn? How easy it would be. *Chop, chop, bleed, bleed, oh what a relief it is.* Was that what troubled them when they closed their eyes? Did they think when they looked at me how much simpler, how much safer, it would have been if I'd never come home from the hospital?

By now Dad and Ned would be home, probably with a good load on. Rodge would have told them that I'd gone crazy again and was out in the woods by myself. And if they started adding things up, if they counted the pills in the bottles, they'd know that Andy-boy had slipped the chains weeks and weeks ago. And, ooohhh boy, would that be scary. Nightmare bloody-ax scary.

So, what would they do? Call in the cops? Call in the National Guard? No, not yet. They'd be too afraid of the Wrath of the Mom to go that far just yet. They'd want to cover up how they'd screwed up. Talk me out of the woods and bundle me quietly off to the hospital. They'd drive the town road, stopping to shout and to blow the horn. They'd make nice, keep the chains and straitjacket hidden until I came out trusting them. If that didn't work, they might try to track me. But even Bern would have trouble doing that. There was just too much country for me to hide in. So then what? Then, my guess was that

Dad would hire Alvin Anderssen's crew and some of the other locals to try to push me out with a long line of drivers like a hunting party driving deer. That could work. Which meant I'd have to get a lot farther into the woods if I didn't want to get caught. That's how I had it figured, anyway. But one thing was for sure, they'd be coming after me in the morning. I wouldn't be walking away anymore, I'd be running.

So I lay in my cave beneath the spruce boughs while the air hung around me, clinging and breathless with the coming of the storm. When I ran fingers through my hair, my skin tingled with static electricity, and I wished I had a mirror to see if my hair gave off sparks of green fire. I pulled the hood of my rain jacket up around my head to keep the mosquitoes out of my ears and dozed, my face damp with sweat.

I came awake, knowing that I wasn't alone. I felt the storm coil, readying itself to spring, and I knew that whatever watched me watched me knowing that I was weak and alone and could not defend myself but could only hide, hoping nothing noticed me. The night seemed to inhale, even the mosquitoes and the frogs going silent. Then the wind came through the trees as if it were not just wind but something living: a mad, rushing thing running berserk through the night forest, crushing everything weak in its way. And I curled up, made myself as small as I could, and felt myself crying though I couldn't hear my sobs over the wind. And I was afraid, afraid, afraid, staring out into the dark, because I could not bear not knowing what watched me, and saw the carrion crows perched along the bare limbs of a dead maple, their wings hunched up as they stared at me with their black, pitiless eyes. And I knew that if I lost my grip even for a second now, the storm would grab hold of the loose end of my sanity, unravel me like a ball of dirty gray yarn. The crows would see to my body, and I would be nothing.

Chapter 10

Birdsong and the smell of rain-washed earth woke me. I crawled out of my cave beneath the spruce and stood shivering in a patch of sunlight. I was tired, stiff, and hungry. God, I was hungry. Yet so much peace surrounded me that it hardly seemed to matter. A breeze blew in the high tops of the trees, swaying the spruce boughs and fanning the leaves of the aspen and birch so that the silver undersides glittered and set the sunlight dancing.

I'd come farther than I thought the night before and stood on a hill high enough to see for a good mile through the gaps in the trees. I could make out the black of the highway to the north and the blue of the river to the east, a half mile beyond the town road. Trees blocked my view to the west, but I knew that another pine swamp blocked any escape that way. To the south lay Balsam Creek and the campsite where I'd fished and talked to Bern. I realized now that I should have crossed the creek last night and headed south where there were miles and miles to roam, instead of heading north and putting myself in a box bordered by creek, swamp, highway, and river. But I was well north of the creek now and back-tracking was too risky.

Yet I was happy that I'd found this high, breezy place, where maybe I could think clearly for a little while. The breeze washed over me, reminding me of how grubby I felt. On impulse I stripped off my clothes, and stood naked and shivering in the wet grass beneath a hemlock until an obliging puff of wind brought down a shower of dew. I washed as well as I could, using my T-shirt as a rag. Then I sat on a fallen log and let the air dry me.

I needed to make some decisions. If I went back to the lodge now, could I talk my way out of going to the hospital? I could tell them that I hadn't really run away last night, that I'd only been trying to get around behind Bern and Rodge so that I could beat them back to the lodge. Kind of a joke, you see. But I'd gotten turned around and had to spend the night in the woods. Would they buy that? Maybe. Oh, Dad would be upset, no question about it. Rodge would be pissed, Ned would be disgusted, and Bern would kind of understand. But if I acted normal, started taking the pills again, maybe I could slide by. "Hey, I'm okay, guys. Just needed a couple of days to think. Don't worry, everything's fine."

Right. Except that pills or no pills, everything wasn't flipping fine at flipping all. As a matter of fact, things were basically more flipping flipped up than flipping ever. So, flip you, flippers, I'm not going back. At that I started giggling, which would have been okay if it hadn't sounded more than a little crazy even to my own ears. Flip you, flippers. Yeah, that was good.

Still giggling, I dug out my topographical map and studied it. Too bad it didn't cover more country, but I still had a way to go before I was off the edge in any direction. Right now, I had to get out of the box where they had some idea of where to find me. Which meant I had to get north of the highway and I had to do it before Dad started recruiting help to search for me. Last night, I'd been pretty sure Dad wouldn't start mounting a real search until I'd had a little more time to come in on my own. But I'd been kidding myself. Rodge would be after him to call in the cavalry. Ned, too, probably. Even now, Dad could be rousting out Alvin and his crew. With a few more locals looking to make a fast buck—and Dad would pay well—there could be a pretty good gang of people looking for me in a couple of hours. But I might not have a couple of hours, because Bern wouldn't wait. He'd go into the woods to track me from my campsite on the creek. It wouldn't be easy even in daylight after the rain, but I wasn't about to bet any money against him.

I dressed, strapped on my belt pack, hooked on my survival kit, and looked around a final time, reluctant to leave. I made myself a promise then. If they caught me—and sooner or later they probably would—I'd remember this place. Through all the drugs they'd give me in the hospital, through all the talk, nodding, and agreeing in therapy, I'd remember. I'd remember even if this time they attached the electrodes and baked my brain like a loaf of bread dough. I'd never tell a soul about this place whatever they did to me. And even if they didn't leave me with much else, I'd have that memory when they finally let me out. Someday, I would come back. I would build a fire and cook bacon and eggs early on a summer morning with the smoke rising with the mist in the first warmth of day.

A flock of maybe a dozen crows winged overhead, and I followed them with my eyes. They didn't pay any attention to me. Different crows, or perhaps there had been no murder of carrion crows on the branches of the dead maple in the night. Quite possible, I told myself. People can see some weird shit sometimes when they're tired and lonely. Don't let it get to you. You've got ground to cover now.

It took me the better part of an hour to get to the highway. I heard car horns a dozen times and shouts that seemed, though they were pretty indistinct, to include the name Andy. Still, I had hope of getting across until I got to the edge of the trees bordering the highway. Old Clyde sat in a lawn chair on the shoulder, maybe a hundred feet away. He seemed quite content, puffing on his old pipe and sipping now and then from an oversized coffee cup. For a half mile either way, he had a clear view. No way was I going to get across unseen. I could go back into the woods, find a good hiding place, and hope that a search missed me. Or I could try to get across the town road and head for the river, where I might be able to swipe a boat or a canoe. But that was dumb. Once I was on the water, someone would see me for sure.

Just then, my luck turned. A mother bear and two cubs decided to cross the highway to Clyde's right. He turned to watch them, and I made a dash for it. I threw myself into the opposite ditch. After a minute, I cautiously peeked through the weeds. Clyde was still sitting in his chair, a lazy curl of smoke rising from his pipe.

I worked my way carefully down the ditch and then crawled for maybe fifty feet into the trees until I was sure he couldn't see me. The land here was a little higher, giving me a good view of the highway and the woods beyond. For the next hour, I watched from behind a tree. Cars passed Clyde, who would wave, as if it were the most natural thing in the world for an old man to be sitting in a lawn chair beside a highway. Several cars I recognized as belonging to locals turned in at the town road, probably carrying people going to help with the search. A car pulled over on the shoulder down by the bridge and parked. Another one parked up the highway to the west. With Clyde in the center, they had the highway covered. Except that I was already across thanks to Ma Bear and her cubs.

I had Dad's plan pretty much figured out by then. Bern had probably been able to follow my tracks well enough to know for sure that I'd headed north. Assuming that I'd made at least a half mile before the storm—and I'd actually done better than that—Dad would send the searchers bushwhacking in along the creek and then turn them ninety degrees to sweep north toward the highway, where Clyde and the other two watchers would spot me the instant I broke cover and sound the alarm. Good plan, as far as it went.

A county sheriff's car slowed to a stop by Clyde. He rose and sauntered over. After a few minutes the deputy waved, started up, and turned in at the town road. Oh, great. Now I was going to have to worry about the law.

I needed to head north, putting as much distance as I

could behind me before dark. I'd begun to think that I really could get away. If I walked maybe fifteen miles a day—a long way in the woods—I could make it to the Michigan border in four or five days. I'd be way beyond the edge of my map, but I still had my compass and a pretty fair idea of the geography. A lot of northern Wisconsin is state and federal forest, miles and miles with only the occasional hunting cabin. I could take shelter in one of those cabins if the weather turned nasty, help myself to a few cans of food, and maybe find a road map. I didn't really want to become a thief, but, hey, desperate times . . . Besides, I wouldn't take anything really valuable.

East of Hurley I would be in the Upper Peninsula of Michigan, nearly three hundred miles of sparsely populated country where I could hike along roads for hours without a car passing. Then finally Sault Ste. Marie and the border with Canada. Getting across would be a problem, but I'd figure out a way. After that, I'd keep going north until the roads ran out. I'd find a lonely cabin in the wilderness and stay the winter. I'd fish, hunt, and gather wild foods. When I turned eighteen, I could come out and there wouldn't be anything they could do to me.

Of course, I could list about a thousand things wrong with this plan, starting with the problem that I had maybe four bucks in my pocket, didn't have a rifle to shoot game—didn't want to shoot game for that matter—didn't have any winter clothes, and on and on. But I could worry about all that stuff along the way. Alternatives? The only one I could think of was trying to hitch to Minneapolis, Milwaukee, Chicago, or some other city. But I'd seen too many TV shows about runaway kids and how they lived in vacant buildings and had to panhandle or sell their bodies to make enough money to eat. I had no desire to hang with them and do what they had to do. I just wanted to be left alone. Well, go for it then, I told myself. Head for the U. P. You don't have to make it to Canada. Not until next spring, anyway. The U. P. is way big enough to hide a few thousand runaway kids. At least get some miles behind you today.

But I didn't move. A girl on a bicycle peddled across the highway bridge from the east side. Izzy. She hesitated at the entrance to the town road, and then continued over to Clyde. They talked, him standing in old-fashioned courtesy. She looked around and, for a second, she seemed to be staring at the spot where I hid.

After a few minutes, she got back on her bike and peddled back down the highway. On the far side of the bridge, she turned left into the side road to Cattail's. And suddenly, I wanted to talk to her, to be with her for just a little while to try to explain everything. Somehow she'd understand. I would go see her tonight after dark. Don't, the sane side of me said. Don't even think about it.

But maybe that was actually the crazy side of me talking. Maybe that was exactly what I should do—see her once more and then call an end to the running. See her and then walk into Cattail's and order a Coke and a hamburger. Yeah, maybe I'd have to go back to the hospital for a couple of weeks. But I knew the ropes. No way was I as crazy as last summer. I'd just stopped taking my pills and gotten a little off the beam. So, I'd take them. Big deal. And when I got out, I could look up Izzy again. With her parents getting divorced, she'd probably spend a lot of time up here this summer. And so what if she was only thirteen? We didn't have to rush things.

Problem: I didn't believe any of this. No, I was too crazy for them to let me out in two weeks. If they ever let me out at all, I wasn't going to be me anymore. I'd crossed the highway, the real one and the one that separated me from any easy way of going back. If I wanted to stay who I was, keep the doctors with their drugs and electrodes from remaking me into what they wanted, I had to get away, had to get to the U. P. and Canada. If I was going to take a chance on seeing Izzy before I left, it could only be to explain why I couldn't stay. Someday I would come back for her.

Another hour passed and a line of searchers straggled out of the woods. Dad was in the middle, Rodge, Ned, and Bern at intervals along the line. No one looked very happy and a general pissed-offedness prevailed. The mood improved when Cattail's pickup pulled up, and he and Izzy began dispensing coffee, sandwiches, and cans of beer. Regular ol' party. I could have put away three or four of those sandwiches myself, that was for sure.

Dad started asking Izzy questions. She shrugged, pointed down the town road where she'd seen me last. How many days ago was that? The deputy sheriff's car came down the road and pulled onto a shoulder near the gathering. The deputy got out, glanced disapprovingly at the beer, which was rapidly gaining popularity from the look of things, and went to talk to Dad. They talked for maybe five minutes, Ned, Rodge, Bern, and Alvin listening in. Then they shook hands, and the deputy headed back to his car. It didn't take Einstein to guess what that had been about: The law was cranking up to get involved big-time. Well, what the hell, it was bound to happen sooner or later. In the meantime, I had to move. But I kept sitting there, watching and wishing I had one of those sandwiches and a chance to talk to Izzy.

When the beer and the sandwiches started running out, Dad and Alvin got the searchers into line east of the town road to push south toward the lodge. Well, have fun, gang. I watched Izzy and Cattail pack up and then finally got going myself. I walked north, angling gradually toward the river. My stomach was grumbling, but I didn't find much in the way of wild plants and berries. A lot of the plants I knew had to be cooked, but I didn't dare start a fire, so I just munched a few I knew were safe to eat raw.

I reached the old highway running down to the one-lane bridge where I'd kissed Izzy, gave the surroundings a good look, and then scuttled across. I worked my way through the trees and brush to the gravel road that ran north along the river for a mile. The DNR had bought up most of the properties along the river, but several hunting cabins still stood on the shore. I looked over each one carefully before passing, though they rarely had occupants except in deer season. When I was upstream a few hundred yards from the old highway, I crept to the shore and rigged a long fishing pole that I could stick over the water while I stayed hidden in the brush.

On the day Bern and I had first fished Huck Finn-style, he'd suggested eating our catch raw. I'd told him no way then, but now a little sushi sounded downright appetizing. Almost immediately I snagged a branch just below the surface. I tried to work the bait free only to break off the tip of my pole, losing one of my three hooks and half my line. Dumb. Still, I needed to catch something, even a redhorse or a bullhead. I rigged another pole, and carefully jigged the bait beneath the surface. No luck.

In the late afternoon, a parade of pickups and battered cars crossed the highway bridge: the searchers giving it up for the day and heading to Cattail's for beer. Maybe twenty minutes later, I heard a car coming slowly up the river road. I ducked deeper into the brush and waited. The car stopped. "Andy! Andy! This is your dad. If you can hear me, come on out, son. It's okay. We'll work everything out." Did I hear whiskey in his voice? I wasn't sure. After a couple of minutes, the car started up and moved on up the road. So they'd guessed that I might be north of the highway now, and I'd wasted my chance to get deep into the woods. Another mistake. Did I want to get away or not?

I heard the car stop twice for Dad to yell before it reached the end of the road and started back. After it passed, I got my bait back in the water, begging for a bite. Still nothing. The river flowed smooth and peaceful. Downstream, the steel skeleton of the old bridge cast its reflection on the river. A good day to be on the river, even if the fish weren't biting. In spite of my hunger and my anxiety, my eyes drooped. Then on the far side of the river, Izzy wheeled her bicycle onto the overgrown landing where Loninger's resort had once stood. I blinked and then jumped to my feet and waved frantically. She didn't see me. I could have yelled—wanted to yell—but the river magnified voices and someone outside at Cattail's might have heard me. She looked up and down the river and then turned to go back to the road. I let my hand drop.

I waited by the river until dusk. I could see the lights of cars crossing the highway bridge and turning in at Cattail's, where Dad was probably standing drinks for Alvin, the crew, and any other locals in the drinking mood. No way could I get across the old bridge to see Izzy until Cattail's closed. Even then it was going to be very risky.

When it was dark, I walked down the river road to the cabin nearest the old bridge. A truck was parked in the yard and a light shone in the window. Damn. I retraced my steps, skipping the next cabin upstream as too close to the first. The third was abandoned, windows gone and waiting for the DNR to send a bulldozer to reduce it to kindling. I looked around inside, using my keychain light, but found nothing useful.

That left only the last and most primitive cabin. I circled it, trying the doors and windows. Everything was locked tight, though it didn't look like anyone had been there for a couple of years at least. Finally, I just started kicking at the back door. It jumped open on the fourth kick. Inside the cabin smelled of dust and mold. A branch as thick as my arm poked through a hole in the roof, and one wall and half the floor were stained dark with rain and mildew. Mouse crap covered the top of the rickety table where mice had chewed the stub of a candle until it was barely more than a wick. I searched the cupboard next to the wood range for food. The mice had done a thorough job of chewing up everything not in cans. I probably could have saved a handful of crumbs (and mouse shit) but remembered Bern telling me about hantavirus, an illness mice carried that was a lot worse than giardia. As in, hantavirus could flat-ass kill you.

Mice had chewed off the labels of the only two cans in the cupboard. The smaller one was probably condensed milk. I had no idea what the bigger one was. Fruit cocktail or peaches, I hoped. I shoved them into the belt pack with my rain jacket, took a last look around, and got the door closed as well as I could. I headed for the woods, my mouth watering at the prospect of opening the cans.

I camped in a grassy spot a couple of hundred yards back from the river road. I used a little of my water to wash the mouse turds off the cans and set about opening them. I had to hold my keychain light in my teeth, biting down to make it shine. A couple of punches with the auger on my Leatherman and I had the condensed milk open. It tasted incredible. I drank it all, tilting the can back until the last drop fell on my tongue. The other can was more of a problem, but I managed to work the appropriate blade halfway around the lid and then pried it up. Pork and beans. I hated pork and beans. I ate them anyway, surprised at how good they tasted. Now to figure out a way to get to Izzy.

Truth was, I'd started building quite a fantasy around Izzy. In it she seemed a couple of years older, her figure fuller, her eyes shy yet inviting. Oh, yeah, quite the babe Izzy. And she was in love with me. Would do anything for me—lie, steal, and have sex. I dozed off thinking of her.

I came awake an hour later, my stomach grinding. I staggered a few feet and barely got my pants and underwear down in time. What came out of me burned all the way through my bowels. I cleaned myself as well as I could with leaves and stumbled back to where I'd been asleep. I was hardly stretched out when I was up again. It came from both ends this time. The third or fourth time my bowels emptied, I started crying. I whined for Mom, for Sylvia, for Dad, even for Rodge.

Maybe the condensed milk and the beans had been too much for my stomach. Maybe I'd eaten something poisonous among the few plants I'd found that afternoon. Or maybe I had giardia. Or hantavirus. Whatever was wrong, I felt like dying. The diarrhea kept returning for hours. When I didn't have anything more in me, my guts still lurched, groaned, and cramped. Somewhere in those hours I began talking to myself. I had a long conversation with Mom, trying to explain why I'd walked away and why I could never go back.

I had questions for her, too. Like why she'd let things go on for so long with Dad's drinking. Why, no matter how hard I tried, she always seemed upset with me. Why hadn't she saved me when the Gloom first started coming?

Things I only barely recalled came back to me. I remembered how, the fall Dad had been treated at Winnebago, she'd told us that he was talking to a psychiatrist named Dr. Bear, and I had an image of a friendly, gentle, storybook bear. I told my dog, Star, about him, and he seemed to like hearing about Dr. Bear curing Dad. Every night after Mom turned off my light, I'd ask God to help Dr. Bear make Dad better. But maybe God had more important things to worry about because Dad didn't get better.

He went back to drinking not long after the New Year's Eve I read *The Mighty Soo* to him. Not openly at first. That would have been too simple in our house. He'd be helping me with my math or something, and suddenly he'd say he had to go down to the basement. If I started to go with him, he'd stop me, tell me to wait, and then hurry down the stairs. Not a lot of brains required to figure that one out.

One night, I found a pint bottle of vodka under a cushion on the couch in the living room. I took it to Rodge. He emptied it down the toilet, and we ran across the street to drop the bottle into a storm drain. Later, I told Mom what we'd done, feeling kind of proud. She sighed and shook her head. "Just ignore the bottles. He has them hidden all over the house."

In my imagination, I saw Dr. Bear lumbering sadly off into the woods to hibernate. Oh, I knew that Dr. Bear wasn't really a bear. But that winter I wanted very much to imagine that he was. Star and I would find his cave and crawl in beside him to sleep warm and safe until spring and better times came.

Chapter 11

Along toward morning, my stomach calmed enough to let me doze for a couple of hours. I woke in the first gray light, feeling a little better but still plenty sick. I had to find a better place to hide until I could get over whatever I had. At the moment, everybody thought I was on the west side of the river, but if I could get to the east side I'd be able to hole up somewhere along the road past the Old Maid's. Later I could try to make contact with Izzy. And then . . . and then I didn't know what the hell what.

I made my way back to the river road and walked south on the edge, trying not to leave any tracks. I ducked back into the woods to skirt the two cabins near the old bridge. At the old highway, I waited for a few minutes, scanning the far shore through the mist rising from the river. I couldn't see anyone watching the bridge, but I couldn't be absolutely sure. I'd have to gamble and be ready to run.

I tried to walk softly, but my footsteps rang on the old bridge. Be casual, I told myself, just a fisherman out early. (Never mind that I had no fishing pole.) I passed the spot where Izzy and I had practiced kissing. At the far end of the bridge, I tried to skirt the narrow upriver side of the pile of gravel that blocked cars from crossing the bridge. Bad move. Years of rain running off the bridge had undermined the blacktop and it buckled under me, tumbling in chunks down the embankment. I followed, sliding down on my ass, my momentum pitching me into a thick patch of cut-grass.

I was alive. Bumped, scraped, and feeling like shit, but alive and apparently still able to move my arms and legs. I crawled shakily up the embankment and peeked around the side of the mound of gravel to see if a crowd of searchers had gathered to laugh their collective butts off. No one. I staggered the few yards to the mouth of the road that ran past the Old Maid's and got under the cover of the overhanging trees.

When I was sure I was safe, I slipped down to the landing where Izzy had stood the night before. I knelt by the river and washed my hands and forearms, the scrapes stinging like hell in the cold water. I had to use the point of the blade on my Leatherman to dig some of the gravel from a deep gouge on my elbow. Fixing myself up took all the bandages and half the tube of antibiotic cream in my survival kit.

I followed the tracks of Izzy's bike to the road. I should leave her a sign, something to tell her that I was alive and wanted to see her. I took a stick and drew an arrow pointing up the road and then scraped a heart beside it with an $A \times I$ in the center. Chances of her seeing it? Practically zip. But at least I'd tried.

The road wasn't much more than a track, though I could tell that two or three cars had been over it since the rain. A partridge thundered up from under my feet, and I dropped to one knee, heart thudding. I had to get a grip. I trudged on, feeling worse with every step. God, what did I have? Did hantavirus hit this fast?

When I got close to the Old Maid's, I slipped into the woods and crept past. But as I came back onto the road, I nearly ran headlong into her. She was standing in a shadow, a fishing pole in one hand, a stringer with three or four small trout in the other. I stumbled back. "I'm . . . I'm sorry. I didn't see you there."

She stared at me for a long moment, blue eyes sharp in the folds of her heavy face. "You're the boy that's runnin'."

"No, no. I'm one of the people looking for him."

A smile bobbed at a corner of her mouth. "No, you're the boy. They even got pictures of you. Your pa stopped and asked if I'd seen you."

"No, really, that's my brother."

"Don't lie to me, boy. What you're doing ain't no never-mind to me. Run till you drop. I don't give a damn."

"You won't tell?"

She snorted. "Who am I gonna tell? Clyde was here last week. He ain't gonna come again for a week or two. And I sure as hell ain't gonna walk down to Cattail's to do your pa any favors. Run all you want. Jus' don't come around my place beggin' for food or nothin'."

"No, ma'am."

She pursed her lips. "Well, you're a polite boy, I'll give you that." She reached in a pocket and pulled out a roll of Life Savers. "Here. That's for being polite to an old lady."

I couldn't have been any more surprised if she'd handed me a fistful of diamonds. "Uh, thanks. Thanks very much. And thanks for not telling anybody where I am."

She chuckled. "I surprised you some, didn't I? Here, give 'em back now. I was just funnin' you."

My heart dropped, but I held out the Life Savers.

Instead of taking them, she slapped her thigh and

laughed. "Good Lord, you are an absolute stitch, boy. Keep 'em. I was just seeing if you're always polite or just some of the time."

I clutched the Life Savers. "I guess I'm mostly polite. Not always. I guess if I really were, I'd turn myself in."

She snorted. "Well, maybe you should, maybe you shouldn't. But I doubt bein' polite has much to do with it. Prove what you gotta prove if it's in you. Or spare yourself the trouble." She started down the road toward her shack but then turned. "There was a girl on a bicycle lookin' for you. Pretty girl. She talked nice to me. If I see her again, should I tell her I seen you?"

"Yes, please. She's a friend."

She nodded slowly. "A friend. Good. Looks like you could use one."

She turned and walked away, the pole on her shoulder. "Thanks again for the Life Savers," I called after her.

I tore open the roll and jammed a cherry, a lime, and a lemon into my mouth. The sugar made me feel almost instantly better. Not great, but better. Sucking on them, I walked on up the track toward the creek, where I guessed the Old Maid had caught her trout. It was still early, the river beyond the trees still smoky with morning mist. The sudden squawk of a loudspeaker on the other side startled me. What the hell? I slipped into the trees to listen.

Whoever was operating the speaker was having trouble getting it adjusted, and it squawked a couple of more times before a voice boomed across the river. "Andrew. Andrew Clanton. This is Sheriff Swanson. I want you to come out from wherever you're hiding. You've caused a lot of people a lot of inconvenience, but we're going to get you the help you need."

I made out the police car on the river road near the old cabin where I'd found the evaporated milk and the pork and beans. The voice paused and then continued. "Now, son, if you don't come out, I'm going to have to send people in to find you. I'm giving you this morning to come to your senses. If you don't, I'll bring in the volunteer fire department. They're not going to be happy about missing work, but they'll come and they'll find you like they've found a lot of lost hunters over the years. And if they can't, I'll bring in a tracking dog and make a couple of my deputies chase after him until he tracks you down."

He paused for a moment, the echo of "tracks you down" still bouncing down the river.

"The harder you make it for us, son, the harder it's going to be for you. If you come out right now, we'll just forget about what it's costing the taxpayers to have me and my men out here. But if you keep running, you'll be going into the juvenile justice system once we catch you.

The judge here doesn't have a lot of patience with young offenders. Chances are he's going to send you somewhere for quite a while, and you'll have a big fine to pay. So give yourself a break and come out."

There was a pause, and then Dad's voice came on. "Andy, just come on out, son. I know you're upset about some things. But we're going to make everything better. I promise, son, we're going to make everything better. Just come out now."

The loudspeaker squawked a final time and went dead. After a minute the car started up and headed down the road toward the old bridge.

I crossed the road and headed east into country I didn't know.

The funny thing was, I might have come out and given up if Dad had just let it alone. I didn't feel good about putting a lot of strangers to a lot of trouble. But then Dad had come on, and I couldn't believe anything he said. Not anymore.

I found that I actually knew a little more of the country east of the river than I'd remembered. A couple of hundred yards in from the road, I came out of the trees into an overgrown field and remembered being there two or three years before with Dad. He'd called the field Gallagher's farm because a lumber company had once had a farm there to grow vegetables for the camps and fodder for the workhorses. In spring and summer, while the lumberjacks drove the logs down the river, the horses grazed in the pasture. I'd liked that picture: the big, hardworking horses resting and growing fat in the summer sun.

The farm buildings had long since disappeared, but the earthen foundations of several old root cellars remained, their sides high except for the openings where the doors had once stood. Small trees had taken root on the sides, shading out the brush that might have grown inside and leaving the floors of the old cellars covered in a thick layer of long grass.

I was pretty well played out, the energy I'd gotten from the Life Savers melting away, leaving me more in need of sleep than ever. The field was too open to be safe for long, but I was still pretty sure that everybody except the Old Maid thought I was on the west side of the river. Could I trust her? Did I have a choice?

A balsam maybe eight feet tall grew in the doorway of the nearest cellar, blocking any easy view inside. I twisted past it and into the shadowy interior. I made a bed in the long grass, turning around a few times like a dog, and lay down with my head cushioned on my rolled jacket. I was dead asleep in seconds.

I slept into the afternoon. I was dimly aware of sounds: bees, birds, a plane passing low overhead, a couple of four-wheelers on the Old Maid's road, the sheriff's loudspeaker once or twice in the distance on the far side of the river. But mostly I just slept, dreaming strange, disjointed dreams. I came awake thinking about Mom and Dad and the afternoon the summer before when I'd gone crazy.

Rodge, Bern, and I were digging out a stump by the old shed up the drive a couple of hundred yards from the lodge. Rodge had sent me to get a pry bar from the garage when Mom's van came bouncing down through the ruts. She stopped and rolled down the window. "How's it going, kiddo?"

"Good, Mom," I said. "How was Girl Scout camp?"

"Oh, it was fun. The kids are having a whale of a time. The older girls keep them rushing from one thing to another. The other women and I just tagged along. I had to look for Sylvia just to say good-bye. She'll be fine on her own. How're things here?"

"Okay," I said. "Except that Dad twisted his ankle the day before yesterday."

"Badly?"

"Not too bad. He's been sitting on the front porch with his foot up and reading."

Her eyes narrowed. "And?"

I shrugged, wanting to tell her and not wanting to tell her. "He's been drinking pretty steady, Mom."

She sighed. "All right. I'll see you later."

The yelling started inside the lodge before I even reached the backyard. I ran in to find Dad standing stark naked in the middle of the main room. He had Mom backed up against the dining room table and he was screaming at her that she had no damned right to tell him what to do. Mom doesn't back down easy, but he had her plenty scared this time.

He spun on me. "What do you want, pencil-dick?"

"Dad—" I said.

"For God's sake, Oscar," Mom pleaded. "Get a bathrobe on. The boys—"

"I don't give a goddamn what they see!" He grabbed his testicles. "Let 'em see what makes a goddamned difference! Who's got the balls. I've got 'em. Not you, not Sylvia, and not Andy, who'd need tweezers to find his. Crying because he shot a goddamned chipmunk, for God's sake! At least I've got one son who isn't a mama's boy pussy!"

"Oscar, Rodger and Bern are just up the road! If they hear you shouting, they'll come down here. Don't make a fool out of yourself in front of them."

"Let 'em see, too! I ain't got nothing to be ashamed of. I am a man! And from now on everybody around here is going to remember that. I'm gonna go naked when I want to, drink when I want to, smoke when I want to, and when I need what you got you'd better be ready, woman!"

At that point I lost it. I ran out the back door, around the side of the garage, and scrambled under the lodge. I crawled my way into the darkness until I was alone and safe among the ancient roots of the great pine stump. I closed my eyes tight, sobbed again for the chipmunk I'd shot just to see if I could hit it. I'd killed him, taken him away from the sunlight and the green earth and every-thing that sang with summer and life. I'd killed him, heard my father say, "Good shot," and felt pride before I'd felt the horror that had turned me sissy forever in his eyes.

Beneath the lodge, I curled up and went away. And I would never have come back if Mom hadn't gone for Rodge and Bern, who crawled in and pulled me out by the ankles.

When I came out of the catatonia in the hospital and started group, the doctor prodded me to tell what had happened. But every time it came my turn to talk, I'd shake my head and go back to staring at the floor. A couple of guys who'd been there awhile started needling me. Frank and Vince liked talking about how messed up they'd gotten on drugs, street crime, and assorted shit. Hell, they were proud of it. Maybe they were a little bored with their act because they kept after me to "come clean," which was a big deal in therapy because no one could get better without "coming clean." Or so the doctor said. Well, screw him and screw them; I wasn't into sharing my problems with anyone.

Then one day, Vince growled when it came my turn. "Ah, what's the use? That pussy ain't gonna say anything."

Frank laughed. "Yeah, no balls at all."

That's what did it. I grabbed my chair and hurled it at them. And I was right behind it, swinging with both fists at those self-satisfied bastards. I swear I would have killed them if two orderlies hadn't pulled me off and held me down while a nurse gave me a shot in the ass that made the world go dark for a long time.

I came to wrapped like a mummy in white sheets with broad belts across my hips and chest holding me to the gurney. I didn't scream or thrash, just lay staring at the softly burning fluorescent light on the white ceiling. Eventually, the doctor came by to tell me that my behavior had "earned me" three days in an isolation room "to think about things." Then a nurse gave me another shot, and I went to sleep again.

I spent the three days figuring out the game. Some guys in the hospital were bullshit artists like Frank and Vince, who'd managed to stay out of jail by getting admitted for treatment.

Some of the guys you saw in the corridors were genuinely crazy, so whacked out on the meds that they couldn't focus on anything. But every so often, you caught something in the eyes of one of them—something desperate that made you wonder. Maybe this one had just been crazy with anger. Maybe he could have fought his way through and come out okay. But the doctors, the nurses, and the orderlies didn't like anger. If you couldn't control it, they hammered you with bigger and bigger doses of drugs until they made you into a zombie who couldn't feel anything at all.

I had a choice: Become a zombie or play the game. So I played the game, made the right noises, and they eased off on the drugs and left me alone, though the anger down deep still chewed on my guts, left me fantasizing in the night about the things I'd do to the orderlies, the doctors, and the nurses if I had them one by one, alone, strapped to a gurney, while this time I had the drugs and worse. Oh, things a lot worse, things jagged, sharp, and cruel.

Chapter 12

The whine of an airplane passing low overhead jolted me back to the present. I peeked out from the shadow of the saplings growing along the walls of the cellar. The plane banked, turning for a run south along the river. I recognized the marking of the fire-spotting plane owned by the DNR. Was it looking for me?

I slid back out of view and thought hard. They were cranking things up. Pretty soon they'd start wondering if I really was on the west side of the river. If they shifted the search to the east side, I'd never get to Izzy. I'd have to run for the Michigan border or just end the whole stinking mess in my own way. Okay, one more try for Izzy and then make some choices.

I thought I'd have to sneak close to Cattail's and try to signal her. But I was lucky. When I hit the road, I saw her wheeling her bike out of the Old Maid's yard. She peddled my way. I didn't want to startle her, so when she was maybe fifty yards away, I stepped into the middle of the road and waved. She stopped abruptly, letting the bike tilt until she caught the weight on her left foot. For a moment she seemed undecided, but then she balanced again and came the rest of the way to me. "I brought you a sandwich," she said.

We sat by the road, eating the cheese and bologna sandwiches. "Take it easy," she said. "You act like you haven't eaten in days."

"I haven't eaten much. Are you going to eat the other half of yours?"

"You can have it. There are potato chips and root beer in the bag. Sorry, but the pop's warm."

"Don't worry about it," I said, digging into the bag. "Did the Old Maid tell you I was up this way?"

"Yes. I don't know why people are so mean to her. I think she's nice."

"Yeah, she's okay."

She hesitated. "So did you leave that heart for me in the road?"

"Huh?"

"The one scraped in the ground."

"Oh, yeah. I left that."

"Including the $A \times I$?"

"Uh-huh."

"Were you being silly?"

"No, I was telling you how I feel."

"Andy loves Izzy?"

"Right."

"But you hardly know me."

"I know you enough. I kissed you, didn't I?"

"After I asked you to." She squeezed her eyes shut and puckered her lips.

"Yeah, but I kissed you the second time because I really meant it."

She thought that over. "Okay. Thanks for the Valentine. It's a little tough to put in my scrapbook, but I liked it."

"You're welcome."

"So, do you want to come back with me now? Maybe we could do something later."

I snorted. "Yeah, like when they let me out of jail or the mental hospital."

She bit her lip. "I heard the sheriff talking to a couple of the guys looking for you. He said you were in the hospital for a while."

"And that I was crazy."

"He said that you were 'troubled.' Are you still kind of, you know—"

"No, I'm not crazy and I'm not troubled. I'm just

pissed at some people and fed up with all their crap. So, to hell with them. I'm going up to the U. P."

"Isn't that a long way?"

"It's not so bad. Fifty or sixty miles. I figure three or four days walking. Maybe five, since I'll have to do some fishing and foraging for edible plants along the way. All you've really got to do is follow the river upstream to the Manitou Flowage and then follow the Pike River until you're almost to the border. You cross the divide there. So, anyway, it won't be too bad a hike."

She glanced speculatively at the woods around us. "Looks to me like it's pretty tough to walk a straight line in the woods. Besides, doesn't the river twist around a lot?"

"Sure. But I've got a compass. I can cut overland to avoid a lot of the bends. And there'll be some dirt roads here and there that I can use as long as I'm careful and don't get spotted."

"Andy—" she said.

But I was getting good and wound up and cut her off. "Have you ever been up to the U. P.? It's really cool. You can just go miles and miles and there's nothing except forest. There are these hunting cabins back in the woods that nobody goes to except maybe a week or two a year. I'm going to find one of those. Then I'm going to fish and hunt and forage and—" I stopped. She was watching me with her clear blue eyes. "And," I said, "I want you to come with me."

She looked startled. "Andy! I'm thirteen. Remember?"

"Yeah, sure, sure. But, hey, it's okay. You'll be fourteen pretty quick, and I'll be sixteen. And in a year we'll be seventeen and fifteen. And then eighteen and sixteen. They can't do anything to me once I'm eighteen. We'll get married. In the old days lots of girls got married at thirteen or fourteen. It'll be okay."

"Andy, you've met me like three times."

"Four times. But I know I love you. Look, I've got this all figured out. We'll walk up to the U. P. We'll need a better map since the one I've got just covers a few miles around here. But if we follow the river we'll be okay until we get a better map. But first maybe you can go back to Cattail's and pack us some food. And get a map, too, if you can. Once we're in the U. P., we'll be safe. We'll probably have to camp out until after deer season, but then we'll find a cabin for the winter and we'll be fine. Next spring, we'll walk the rest of the way to Sault Ste. Marie. I haven't exactly figured out how we're going to get across the border yet, but I'll come up with something. And once we're in Canada, we'll be twice as safe. We can get jobs for the summer. We can cut grass. I'm good at that, and nobody cares who you are if you're just cutting grass. I read a book about this kid who gets stranded at this bus station when he's real little. He's so shy he doesn't say anything, and people start thinking he can't talk. And he figures out playing the deaf-mute is a good act because nobody hassles him. Instead, people give him food and a place to stay and hire him to do odd jobs. So he's got everything he needs and decides he'll just keep playing the deaf-mute. I can be like him. You can do the talking, tell people I'm your brother and that our parents are dead or something. They'll give us jobs, and we'll make a lot in tips because people will feel sorry for us. By fall we'll have enough money saved to buy supplies. Then it'll just be finding another hunting cabin for the winter."

I was talking way too fast, all the words, ideas, and fantasies just pouring out of me. I jumped to my feet. "Come on! I'll explain on the way. You don't have to go back to Cattail's for food. We'll just go now." I grabbed her hand and pulled her to her feet.

"Andy, stop! You're not making any sense. We're just kids. We can't walk all that way to Canada. We can't live out in the woods by ourselves. We'll run out of food. Suppose one of us gets sick? And I could, like you know, get pregnant."

"We can deal with all that. Even having a kid. I'll be a good father. You'll see. I know everything that parents can do wrong and I won't do any of them. I'll . . . I'll make one of those baby slings. You can carry him in that. And I'll take my turn. We'll be good parents. As long as we love each other and love him, everything will be okay. You'll see."

She closed her eyes tight, two tears sliding down her cheeks. I hesitated and then leaned forward to kiss them away. She put up her hands to stop me. "Don't," she said.

"Izzy, just believe in—"

"Stop it, Andy!" She tried to get control of her voice. "Look, I think you're about the nicest guy I've ever met. But, Andy, you're talking crazy. I can't go with you. I'm too young, and I don't want to go. You need to come back with me. Cattail likes you. He won't let them do anything bad to you. You can eat supper with us and have a shower and then . . . and then maybe you can talk to somebody who can help you figure things out."

"Come with me," I pleaded. "I love you."

"No!"

I grabbed her hand again. "We'll talk about it on the way. Come on. We just have to follow this road up the river and then swim across above the big bend where the river swings east. It'll be okay. I'll protect you. I'll carry you if I have to."

"Andy, no! I can't. I've got no reason to go!"

"I can be the reason. I'll be the reason. I'll love you." I started pulling her toward the road.

"No!" she yelled, pulled her hand free, and ran.

"Izzy!" I shouted. "Izzy, come back."

She turned. She was sobbing, her face red and scrunched up like a frightened little girl's. "Andy, you need help! You're sick. Just wait here. I'll bring Cattail. He won't hurt you."

Then she was running again.

"But your bike . . . ," I said weakly, as if her old bike made any damned difference.

I stumbled north, tears blinding me. Every one had turned against me. Even Izzy. I should have been calculating instead of crying, running instead of walking. I had maybe twenty minutes before Izzy reached Cattail's and told people where I was. But her betrayal was all I could think about.

The whine of engines jerked me back to reality. I dived for the side of the road, scrambled up the bank, and lunged into the brush. I was barely out of sight when two four-wheelers swept around a curve to the south and came on very fast. The riders rode hunched forward over their handlebars—a couple of crew-cut guys who might have been firefighters or even National Guard. They had my trail, and their eyes were slitted and hungry like wolves' eyes. They might have been running down a tired deer. I wasn't a person anymore—I was prey.

And I was a goddamned idiot, too. Not everybody searching for me was a fool. A few might suspect that I'd slipped across the river, and these two had gone to have a look at the road past the Old Maid's. And what did they find? A thirteen-year-old girl running down the road, crying her eyes out—a girl probably everybody in the county knew was my friend. Two minutes of questioning her and it was: "Hit the gas, Charlie! We've got him now!"

Not quite yet. I crashed through the brush. The crows were back, perched in the trees, cawing and cawing as I ran past. At the edge of what had been Gallagher's farm, I took a hasty look over my shoulder for the plane, and then ran dodging among the old cellars. My survival kit banged against my waist and brush grabbed at the belt pack containing my rain jacket and water bottle. I had to get south of the highway before the sheriff could shift the search to this side of the river. My stomach lurched and everything I'd eaten bolted for the nearest exit. I sprawled on my hands and knees, puking and then puking again, vomit splattering my hands and arms. I tried to wipe the vomit off in the grass but only smeared it worse. You're just about run to death, man, a voice in my head told me. But then I was stumbling on. Not yet, not if I could get south of the highway.

I still had enough sense to slow down when I got a glimpse of the highway through the trees. Anything running through the woods makes a lot of noise, even a squirrel, and I'd made plenty. I crept the last dozen yards as quietly as I could and peered out. Not twenty yards away a big pickup with a gum ball on the dash stood on the opposite shoulder. An old guy I didn't recognize leaned against the front bumper, smoking a cigar and looking bored. Every minute or so, he'd glance over his shoulder, but it didn't look like he was taking his job very seriously.

I'd just about gathered my strength for a sprint across the highway the next time he looked away when I heard the roar of heavy engines coming from my left. Three Harleys topped the hill to the east and came thundering toward us. I ducked low as they slowed to a stop by the pickup. The riders were the real thing: meaty, bearded guys in black leather and jeans. "Hey, man," the leader shouted over the roar of his engine. "Down here where they got free beer if you spend some time lookin' for a lost kid?"

The old guy pointed down the road. "Turn in at Cattail's. Someone there will give you the word."

The three guys gunned their bikes and roared off,

the old guy watching them go. I made my move then, the roar of the bikes covering the sound of my feet as I sprinted across the highway. In the brush I turned to see if I'd made it without getting caught. The old guy glanced at his watch and then at the sky, leaned against the front bumper of his truck, and got his cigar going again.

I rested for a few minutes. The DNR plane swept low along the highway. The old guy by the pickup raised a hand, and the plane dipped its wings. I'd about caught my breath when I heard the sirens. On the far side of the river, two sheriff's cars, lights flashing and sirens screaming, roared out of the side road leading to the old bridge. Dad's Ford was hot behind them. They crossed the highway bridge and turned in at Cattail's road, disappearing behind the trees. I could hear them passing Cattail's and then slowing to take the dirt road to the Old Maid's. I could almost see the old guy itching to join the action. Go ahead and go, you old fart, I thought. You've already screwed up what you were supposed to be doing here. I ain't up there anymore.

I picked my way through the woods, staying off Shadpole Lane, which ran south past a couple of vacation cabins near the river before swinging east to make a long loop back to the highway. Once upon a time the lane had led to a couple of resorts, but they were long gone, bought by the DNR and knocked down in its program to expand the state forest. When Bern still had his four-wheeler, we'd run up and down the road a few times and I'd walked it more than once on my own. If I could make it to the point where the lane swung east, I could follow an old driveway down to the river not far above the point where the lodge sat atop the ridge on the opposite side. And then . . . well, I'd know that when I got to the river.

In all my running, scrambling, and puking, I'd never thought to drink until I was south of the highway. But when I felt for my water bottle, the lump it made in my belt pack was missing. I couldn't remember when I'd had it last, but it was gone now. And I was screwed. If I hadn't gotten giardia before I'd get it now. I felt big tears well in my eyes. Hold on, hold on, I told myself. You've still got your purification tablets. You've still got your Sierra cup. But I had no water and didn't know where I could find any until I got back to the river.

I spent the night in a clump of spruce trees. The mosquitoes found me, didn't seem to mind at all when I rubbed repellent on my face and hands. No-see-ums bored in, even less impressed. I got on my rain jacket, hid every inch of skin I could, but still they found me. I drowsed, my back to a tree trunk. Every so often a car or a pick-up would cruise slowly along the lane. A couple of times I heard the squawk of a police radio and once I saw a searchlight beam trying to penetrate the brush.

I suppose I might have dozed off now and again, but no one is ever going to convince me that I was asleep or hallucinating when the crows and the other creatures came. The crows hopped and strutted around me, eyeing me with their black, pitiless eyes. The others watched and waited: a pair of timber wolves, a bobcat perched on a limb, a weasel or perhaps a mink up on its hind legs and peering over the weeds, and farther back still, a knot of nervous coyotes, anxious to scatter the crows and have at me but hesitant in the presence of the big wolves, who would take the choicest parts of me.

Chapter 13

I awoke knowing exactly what I had to do. I couldn't make it to the U. P. now that Izzy had told them my plan. And I couldn't turn myself in, hoping to get off with a month or two of faking my way through therapy. By now they would have dragged Izzy over her story a dozen times, twisting it until I came out looking like a rapist. In my heart, I knew I'd never meant to scare or hurt her. But I'd frightened her plenty with my crazy talk and then terrified her when I'd tried to pull her along with me. By now even she would be thinking the worst of me.

Amateur hour was over. The sheriff would be calling in the state police and every deputy he could beg from surrounding counties. They weren't chasing a "troubled" kid anymore, they were hunting down a child molester. They'd post deputies or state police on every road north, south, and east, and then push a posse west through the woods until I was pinned against the river, helpless to get away as the circle tightened until they had me. Then Dad with all his legal skills and Mom with all her tears wouldn't be able to save me. I was going down hard.

I knew a secret that Dad had never figured out: Northerners hated city folks. They'd take our money in their bars and restaurants, tax the hell out of us for our cottages on the river, but basically they didn't like us. Dad could buy them all the drinks he wanted to, call everybody from Alvin Anderssen to the county judges by their first names, but none of that bought us respect. Given a chance, they'd turn on us like a pack of pissed-off rottweilers. I was that chance. I'd screwed with them and now they were going to screw me.

I'd gone to court with Dad a couple of times to see him argue a case, and I could picture him arguing to get me off with probation or supervision or something. But I could also picture the judge—gray, old, and sly— slapping down every argument before staring coldly at me. Guess what, sonny? You're going to the juvenile reformatory at Lincoln Hills. And that's in our backyard. Our people do the guarding, and a few of our tough lads just happen to be guests of that excellent facility. And they're going to knock that city crap out of you. So brace up, sonny. It's a long time until you're eighteen.

Yeah, Lincoln Hills, where I'd meet some of the real bad guys—guys who'd beat the shit out of me and then spread-eagle me facedown on a cot so they could screw me up the ass. I'd come out at eighteen a pathetic little wuss so afraid of everything that I'd never get right or even straight again.

Even if I got lucky enough to go back to the hospital, this time I'd go to the lockdown wing where they'd hit me with the heavy stuff, the stuff that turned angry guys into zombies. And if the drugs didn't do it, they'd connect the electrodes, blow the top of my head off with electricity so that I wouldn't remember how to wipe my own ass by the time I got out—if I ever got out at all.

I knew Mom and Dad would work their tails off to get me sent to the hospital instead of Lincoln Hills. If they'd work to get me out was another question. I was the disappointment, the sissy. Why bother to get me out at all? Oh, the neighbors would talk some. But, hey: "Out of sight, out of mind." Better to put up with some gossip for a few weeks than have me around as a permanent embarrassment. Time to move on, get the priorities straight, concentrate on the two kids who had the ol' right stuff.

So there it was. I was about to get caught and screwed. Unless, that is, nobody had thought of one small detail. And I was pinning all my hopes on that one chance.

I worked my way south through the woods. Behind me I could hear car and truck doors slamming along the highway and the sheriff's bullhorn directing everybody to gather for a briefing. North, I thought. Just go north first. Just give me one lousy hour.

The sheriff wasn't putting all his money on any one direction, and several four-wheelers and cars cruised down Shadpole Lane in the next hour. But all was silent when I reached the curve. A solitary vacation cabin stood off to the left, no car in the driveway and the curtains drawn. I didn't give a damn about food anymore, but I was desperate for a drink of clean water. I circled the cabin to make sure it was really vacant and then kicked in the back door. It was quiet and clean inside, the air still and floating with dust motes in a streak of light coming through a gap in the curtains. I ducked my head under the kitchen faucet, drinking my fill and then letting the water run over my hair and face. God, I could use a shower, but I was about to get very wet anyway.

I walked through the cabin, munching on some crackers I'd found in the kitchen cupboard. Nice place. I mean, really nice. I poked into cupboards and drawers, not really looking for anything, although yesterday I could have thought of a hundred things I needed. Maybe I'd take a gun if I found one. Yeah, I could scare the shit out of some people if I found a gun. Go out in a blaze of glory. *Come and get me, coppers!*

I opened the door of a cupboard set a little away from the wall. It was filled with glasses and the slight vibration of a couple of them gave me my first warning. I stopped breathing, heard very faint pings coming through the back panel of the cupboard—a phone dialing. I looked frantically at the cupboard door, saw the little square in the corner, and knew instantly that it was an alarm sensor. I jerked it loose and crushed it beneath my heel. The phone kept dialing. Shit! How many of these damned things had I tripped? Did it matter? Not a goddamned bit. A panel was lighting up in the sheriff's department or the security firm. Hell, for all I knew, it could be lighting up at Homeland Security in Washington. But somewhere, somebody was making a call. Message to sheriff: Your boy is a mile south of Highway 70 on Shadpole Lane breaking into a cabin. Go get him!

I hit the door running. I was across the lane in seconds. I had one thing left in my favor. They didn't know where I was going, but I did, had known since sometime in the night, and what I was going to do when I got there.

I sprinted down the overgrown driveway to where

Shadpole resort had stood before the DNR had bought and bulldozed it. Behind me a siren wailed. Subtle these guys weren't. I took the rotting wooden steps down to the old dock two at a time, pausing only long enough to scan the river both ways. Just as I'd figured, the sheriff had put a boat halfway between the highway bridge and the lodge. The guy in the boat scanned the shoreline, sunlight flashing off the lenses of his binoculars. There'd be another boat above the old bridge, and probably a third downstream of the bend half a mile below the lodge. What I hoped no one had considered was the short stretch of fast water between the low rapids on either side of the bend. That was my escape hatch, my one way out of this mess.

The narrow floodplain gave me a strip of fairly open ground where I could move fast. I jogged along it, the alder brush and cedar along the shore keeping me pretty well hidden from the river. If the guy in the boat upstream really had his shit together, he might spot me through the gaps, but I was gambling that he'd be focusing his attention on the sound of sirens moving rapidly down Shadpole Lane. Still time, I thought. With just a little luck, still time. I glanced toward the river, saw a crow flapping easily along with me. No murder of crows anymore, just the one now. My crow. My friend.

I passed the point where I could see the lodge on the

low ridge across the river, passed the point where Balsam Creek flowed into the river from the west, and paused to rest when I could see the rapids on either side of the bend and the strip of open fast water between. If there was another boat below the lower rapids, I couldn't see it. I walked the rest of the way to the bend and sat down on the shore. In the river between the rapids, the tops of a few of the old bridge pilings still poked above the water where the logging railroad had crossed the river eighty or a hundred years before.

The rapids themselves weren't any big deal, just short rips that became "rock gardens" in low water. Getting a fishing boat through them was a major hassle, but anybody with any skill could slide a canoe through, no sweat. But the sheriff wouldn't have posted canoes. No, he'd have posted boats and that left me the hundred yards where they couldn't get at me in the time it'd take me to get across. The water wouldn't be much over my thighs until I got to midstream, where I might have to swim a little.

I'd anticipated having to strip in the brush and then plunge in, moving fast before they saw me. But I was now hidden from the boat upstream and still couldn't see another one downstream. Time enough to do things right for once.

Unbuckling my belt pack, I let it drop and then

stripped off my shirt, boots, and jeans. I opened the blade on my Leatherman and sliced off the legs of my jeans above the knee. I unrolled my Gore-Tex rain jacket and slit it in three places across the back. Finally, I made three holes with the punch in the bottom of my Sierra cup and three more in the cover for good measure. I stood, wound up, and threw the Leatherman as far as I could. I sent my survival kit after it, watched it hit the water and float down into the lower rapids, slowly sinking. My Gore-Tex jacket, my Leatherman, and my survival kit they couldn't have. They were welcome to the rest.

I pulled on the shorts I'd made out of my jeans and laced up my boots. Somewhere on the far side, I'd abandon the boots, too, go the rest of the way barefoot in just my shorts. But not naked. No, I'd leave naked until the very last. Now it was time to leave everything else behind. Time to cross the river and finish what I'd set out to do.

I double-knotted my boots and stood for a moment in the warm sunlight, not caring who spotted me now. Then with everything discarded on the bank, I waded into the river to cross to the far shore and the great swamp where I'd spent the first night of my walkaway. In the swamp I'd stretch out naked under the open sky to eat a bulb of poison hemlock. The swamp would welcome my body, embrace it, dissolve it, hide me forever. I would live on only in dreams and stories: the maniac kid who'd disappeared into the great pine swamp. Around fires, camp counselors would scare city kids with tales of me. In bars, hunters would claim to have heard and seen strange things in the woods. At dusk, cross-country skiers would glance over their shoulders to see if a shadow slipped along with them. For a few years, there would be those who knew enough to correct the exaggerations, but before long people would forget the truth. I would live on in the places people feared to go, the dark and swampy places where things rotted and sprouted in the moonlight, slithered and hopped, swooped low and taloned on silent wings. And when even the stories grew old and faded away, I would become legend, a creature that prowled muddy roads in warm spring dusks, left tracks across dewy grass on summer dawns, rattled the windows on autumn evenings, and howled on winter nights when the wolves and the northern lights danced in snowy woods.

Chapter 14

Maybe my story should have ended there. When I stepped into the river, I'd answered all the questions, made all the choices, and knew exactly what the ending should be. In a way, I've always regretted that there turned out to be so much more to the story, since certainty is so hard to come by and I've never been so certain of myself or anything else in my life before or since.

I waded until I had to swim and swam until I could wade again. I climbed out onto a low shelf of rock that had supported one end of the old railroad trestle before time and spring floods had carried it away. I undid my boots, emptied the water out, and pulled them on over my bare feet. Something behind me snorted, and I whirled to see the biggest creature I'd ever seen standing in the shadow of the trees at the edge of the old railroad cut. For a moment I had the irrational thought that it was a moose, although the last moose in Wisconsin had been shot over a century before.

The creature moved, coming into the sunlight, and I saw that it was Sally, one of Alvin Anderssen's work-horses. Clyde sat on her bare back. He smiled at me, his lined, weathered face kind. "Hey there, Andy. Looks like you're getting chewed on some."

I brushed away the half dozen mosquitoes that had landed on my chest. "Clyde! What are you doing here?"

"Oh, the sheriff didn't need an old coot like me. So Sally and me just set out to see if we could find your trail on our own. Found a couple of the places where you'd camped. And I talked to Maggie yesterday. She said she'd seen you and that you looked a little peaked but okay. She said she gave you a roll of Life Savers."

So Maggie was the Old Maid's name. "Yeah, she was nice."

"Yep. Maggie's okay. We've always gotten along fine. One of these days I might just move in with her."

"How'd you find me here?"

"Just a lucky guess. I thought you'd try to get back on this side of this river where there's more room to roam. I've taken the horses across here and figured you might choose it. So, where are you headed now?"

"Into the swamp."

"Skeets are awful bad in there. You'll get et up."

I didn't say anything. Sally ducked her head and began cropping grass. Clyde pursed his lips. "I think maybe you ought to climb up behind me. Sally and I'll take you home."

"I can't do that, Clyde. I've got a plan all worked out."

He nodded slowly. "Well, I guess we'll just mosey along with you then. See that you don't get in no trouble."

I could hear shouts on the other side of the river, looked and saw men coming through the woods. "I've got to go, Clyde. And I've got to go alone."

"I don't know that I can let you do that, Andy. The other day when you sneaked across the highway while I was watching the bears—"

"You saw me?"

"Yep. You ain't exactly quiet in them boots."

"But why didn't you yell or something?"

"Oh, I figured you was running for a reason and that you'd stop when you was ready. Weren't my business."

"That's the same thing the Old Maid said."

He nodded. "Well, like me, she figured you'd come out when you was ready." He turned, listened. "There's another bunch coming in from the road. Looks like you're pretty well trapped. Come up behind me. We'll go meet them."

"I can't, Clyde."

He fished in a breast pocket and pulled out one of the FRS radios. He gazed at it quizzically. "Your pa gave me this. Don't exactly know how to use it, though." He held it out to me. "Maybe you should call him."

For a second, my hand almost reached for the radio. Then I said, "I can't. Please just let me go."

He shook his head. "I owe your pa for a lot of favors, Andy. Some work when there wasn't any other around. A couple of times he lent me money. It was him who set it up for Cattail to keep my Social Security on account so that Alvin and the rest of them didn't drink it up."

"There he is!" somebody shouted from the far shore.

"Clyde, I've got to go."

"Can't keep you from going. Sally and me will just come along with you."

"That'll ruin everything."

He looked over his shoulder again. "Boys coming from the road will be here in a few minutes. Doubt that you can get by them now. Maybe we should just wait here. Breeze will keep a few of the skeets off you, anyway."

And that's what we did. We waited. By now a dozen men had come out of the woods on the far side of the river. They spread out along the shore and stood or hunkered down to watch. The crow landed in a tree near us, tilted his head one way and then the other, studying me. Then he cawed once, hopped into the air, and took wing. That was the last time I saw him.

Five minutes later, the searchers began appearing from the woods behind Sally and Clyde. At first they were excited, then turned hesitant, standing in a thickening semicircle at the edge of the woods. A pair of four-wheelers bounced down the old railroad cut through the forest. Dad rode behind a short, gray-haired man in uniform who I guessed must be the sheriff. Rodge rode behind Bern on the other.

Dad got shakily off the four-wheeler and came toward me. Oh, hell, he couldn't be! But he was, all right. Drunk as a frigging skunk. I couldn't handle it. I spun and plunged for the river. I'd dive, hope I'd break my neck on a rock. And if I didn't, I'd let the current take me downriver until I drowned.

"Andy!" Dad yelled, and tried to run after me.

And I stopped, stood balanced on the slippery rock ledge at the edge of the river. "What, Dad? What?"

"I'm sorry! God, I'm so sorry. Just don't hurt yourself. We'll get you some help. Make everything okay again."

Okay *again*? When had it ever been okay? I could have told him that he was the one who needed help. Maybe I could have made a bargain with him. Hope that he could stop drinking for good this time. But it was at that point that he lost his balance on the slippery ledge and tumbled into the river. And I just watched him go under, not caring any longer what happened to him.

It was Bern and one of the deputies who went in to fish him out. The sheriff sauntered up to me in the commotion. "I think you'd better come along with me, son."

I turned on him, pointed to where Bern and the deputy were dragging Dad onto the shore. "Do you see that? Do you see what I've had to live with?"

He nodded. "I see it. But you won't be going back home for a while. You've broken some laws and now you need to come with me."

"I'm never going back to live with him."

"That'll be up to the judge and people from Social Services. My job is to take you in. So, come on. You can ride on the back of the four-wheeler."

"Aren't you going to cuff me?"

"Your wrist to my belt. That's just procedure. No way around it."

I hesitated. "Can I ride with Clyde? Just through the woods."

He pursed his lips. "You going to run?"

"I haven't got anyplace to go."

"No, you don't. Not that we won't find you. Okay, go ahead."

So I climbed up behind Clyde on Sally's broad back, and we rode through the crowd of searchers and through the green woods on either side of the old railroad cut to where the sheriff's mud-spattered Ranger stood on the road. "Must be a good truck," Clyde said. "Ain't too much that can make it this far."

"I know," I said. "It's kind of tough back in here."

Epilogue

The sheriff took me to the emergency room at the hospital in Chelles, where a doctor checked me over and said that except for some dehydration I'd survived pretty well. Then the sheriff shook my hand, wished me good luck, and turned me over to a couple of his deputies. They drove me to a hospital in Wisconsin Rapids for a seventy-two hour evaluation on the mental wing. At that point, I crashed. For three days, I slept, ate, answered as many questions as I had to, and then slept again.

On the third day, Mom and Dad met with the shrink. An orderly brought me in, and I sat there in my white gown and powder blue bathrobe and listened while the shrink told them that he was going to recommend that the judge send me to the mental hospital where I'd been the summer before. They didn't object. I didn't object. What was the point?

My time in court took slightly longer than most people take to brush their teeth. I had quite a few charges against me, including trespass, disturbing the peace, breaking and entering, theft, fleeing an officer, and sexual assault. The assistant DA asked the judge to drop the sexual assault charge because he'd received a letter from Izzy saying that nothing had happened. The judge agreed to that and then read a couple of paragraphs out loud from the shrink's evaluation of my "mental state" and a couple more from the report by the social worker. Summary, I was one badly screwed up kid who might do himself or someone else harm. Finally, he turned to me. "Do you have anything to say, young man?"

"No, sir," I said.

He gazed at Mom and Dad. "Mr. and Mrs. Clanton, I'm not sending your son to jail, but I'm not sending him home either. If you're not going to argue for that, you can say whatever you want."

Neither one of them had anything to add.

"Very well," the judge said. "With the State's agreement, the court sets aside the charges against Master Clanton, pending treatment of his mental condition at the state hospital at Mendota." He went through a bunch of stuff about how the court would have custody of me while I was in treatment and so on. Then a rap of the gavel, a quick hug from Mom and a handshake from Dad, and I was off to the hospital for drugs, treatment, and general jacking around.

But it worked out better the second time. My roommate, Gary, came in about the same time, and we got along pretty well from the start. At first they pumped a lot of drugs into us, him because he liked to set fires, me because I was just generally nuts. We shared a therapist, a young guy who didn't look that much older than Rodge and Bern, although I suppose he was at least thirty. He said to call him Chuck and turned out to be pretty cool.

I figured I'd just play the therapy game like the last time, but after a couple of weeks, Chuck started getting it through my head that not all my problems came from "family issues."

"Wait a damned second," I said. "Are you telling me that the problems are all in my head? That my family had nothing to do with them? Because that's bullshit, man."

Chuck shrugged his shoulders. "No one knows how all the physiological and environmental stuff fits together. There are new theories every year, most of them a lot of hooey. Let's just say you're more susceptible to external pressures because you've got some imbalances in your brain chemicals."

"And so you want me to take a bunch of drugs so I'm not me anymore."

"Nope, you're going to be more of who you really are. And I like to call them medications."

"Well, I like to call them drugs."

He shrugged his shoulders again, smiled his easy smile. "Call 'em what you like. But they work. Trick is you've got to take them."

"And then I'm going to be just fine, huh? No problems at all?"

"Nope, didn't say that. But you'll handle your problems better."

"Don't patch me up just so I can go back to live with them. Because I'm not going."

"Where you live will be the court's decision. But I can tell you one thing for sure—you're not going anywhere for a while. Might as well make good use of your time here."

I stared stubbornly at him. "No pills."

He smiled. "Okay. Your choice."

The next day I told him I'd try the pills. Truth was, I'd been told a lot of the same stuff the summer before, but I hadn't been ready to listen then.

Every night before lights-out, a couple of orderlies would come in and toss our room to make sure Gary hadn't scored any matches. But one night they missed a pack Gary had filched from one of the nurses' purses. He lay on his bed, caressing the matches with a thumb. "I'd sure like to start a fire," he said. "Not, you know, a big one. Just a trash can or something."

"Why, Gary?"

He shrugged. "I don't know. I just like fires."

"It's gonna screw you up with Chuck."

He sighed. "I know. I'd just like to set one more. Then I'd quit. Really quit."

I didn't say anything.

Finally, he turned to me and held out the pack. "Would you take care of these for me?"

"I could do that." I went down the hall to the bathroom, tore the matches out of the pack, and flushed them down a toilet.

At first the hospital social worker said I'd probably get out after a couple of months when I was "stabilized." But Chuck said I was too "fragile," and it wasn't until January I got out for good.

I'd had a couple of home visits and quite a few letters by then. (No Internet and no e-mail for us crazy folks. Shit, we might learn how to make a nuclear bomb or start threatening the president.) Mom wrote every other day, Sylvia always adding a few lines on the bottom. Dad's first letter was the longest he sent—all about how sorry he was for this and that but that I had to understand . . . blah, blah. I wasn't interested.

I got a couple of notes from Dick and Bern and a longer one from Rodge. He made a half-assed apology for leaving me alone with Dad the weekend I went crazy. I wrote back and told him to forget it. Sooner or later it was bound to happen, that was just the weekend it did.

Izzy wrote, which was exciting since part of me still imagined that we had the beginning of something special. They were nice enough letters, mostly full of girl stuff about clothes, hair, and makeup—stuff that she'd apparently started to care about. She sent me a picture of her and her date dressed up for the homecoming dance. I wrote her back, telling her that she looked fantastic and to make guys treat her right. She wrote a couple of times after that, but I guess she'd run out of things to talk about, and I guess I had, too. She signed her last letter "Love always, Isabelle." Not Izzy. Not anymore.

What happened after I got out of the hospital? Well, I'll give you a choice and you can select the ending you like.

Scenario 1: Dad got his shit together, quit drinking, and started going to AA meetings two or three times a week. Mom stopped being so tense, and everything at home smoothed out. Rodge and I became best buddies over spring break and even spent a weekend alone at the lodge having a hell of a good time. Sylvia and I grew closer, too, sharing secrets and giggling at "inappropriate times." Dusty actually started to like me. Bern and Dick did great. I got a girlfriend named Shiva (hippie parents). I never walked away again.

Scenario 2: Dad tried but couldn't stop drinking, and Mom filed for divorce. He moved out of the house to an old apartment on the north side of Brunswick. His partnership with Ned broke up, and Dad practiced law out of a tiny office with only a part-time secretary. Rodge went off to Yale. He e-mailed Mom, didn't e-mail me. We saw him quite a bit the winter Mom, Sylvia, and I moved to Hartford, Connecticut, which is practically within spitting distance of New Haven and Yale. Mom went to work in state government, quickly making herself indispensable. I couldn't live with her. We fought all the time, and after I'd taken off a couple of times she quit trying to make me live at home. Social Services put me in a group home, which was a definite improvement. Every couple of nights I'd have a conversation with Sylvia by Instant Messenger. She was growing up, and we got to like each other better.

Going crazy cost me a year in school. But once I went back I did well enough to graduate in the top third of my class from West Hartford High—not good enough for Yale, of course, but good enough for some other things. Rodge is still at Yale. Bern is still studying to be a forester. I've kind of lost touch with Dick. (He took Dusty when our family broke up. They like each other, which is good.) Sylvia and Mom are doing fine. I don't keep in touch with Dad. Sorry, no Shiva. No steady girlfriend at all, but I've had some good times.

So there you have it. Take your choice.

I'm graduating from high school tomorrow. I'm nineteen and I'm doing okay. It's been one hell of a bumpy road at times, but now that I've made it this far I figure I'll see what's up ahead. College maybe, but I'm thinking of tech school.

I've never been back to that breezy hill where I woke on the morning after the storm. But I'll get there someday. If I meet the right person, I may take her along. My other fantasy, the one where I'm standing on the high point of one of those big lake boats out of Sault Ste. Marie, watching the lock gates swing wide and the great lake opening in front of me, clear and blue all the way to the horizon . . . Well, I might just get there, too. I kind of think I will.

So, anyway, that's it. Thanks for coming along. Take care. Be cool. And pack your survival kit. You never know when it might come in handy.